The Mona Lisa Mirror Mystery

LATAYNE C. SCOTT

Into the Art Series, Book 1

Cruciform Fiction

Dedicated to young readers, who are my hope for the future.

The Mona Lisa Mirror Mystery

Print / PDF ISBN: 978-1-949253-03-0
Mobipocket ISBN: 978-1-949253-04-7
ePub ISBN: 978-1-949253-05-4

Published by Cruciform Press, Minneapolis, Minnesota. Copyright © 2018 by Latayne C. Scott.

This is a work of fiction. Names, characters, businesses, places, events, locales, and incidents are either the products of the author's imagination or used in a fictitious manner. Any resemblance to actual persons, living or dead, or actual events is purely coincidental.

"Christian fiction at its finest!"
　Shelly Beach, Christy Award-winning author

"Crosses space and time…*The Mona Lisa Mirror Mystery* is for the lover of mysteries and art."
　Patti Hill, author, *The San Clemente Bait Shop*; *Telephony*

"A book your teen won't want to miss…I will recommend it over and over."
　Celeste Green, Academic Dean, Oak Grove Classical Academy

"So imaginative, so engaging. Well done."
　Sharon K. Souza, author, *What We Don't Know*

"The characters are well developed and the plot has a way of drawing you directly into the action. I can't wait to read the next one."
　Joy Capps, reviewer, HomeSchoolLiterature.com

"*Mona Lisa* is a L'Engle-ish blend of family, fantasy and adventure, friendship, and deep wisdom."
　Kathleen Popa, author, *To Dance in the Desert*; *The Feast of St. Bertie*

"May we all…*whoosh* away into lives full of truth, art, and life-enriching thoughtful abandon."
　Stephen Collins, Associate Headmaster, Riverbend Academy

Chapter One

So my dad always told me, from the time I was little, that a woman reached the full bloom of her beauty at age sixteen. Of course that led to another discussion about being perfect in heaven. And if someone died before that time, would they be sixteen forever in heaven?

Or on the other hand, did all old women regress to age sixteen at the pearly gates? (But Dad usually chickened out on that one—I think the idea of all teenagers in heaven made him nervous.)

Long story short, I kept that in my mind all my life, about becoming sixteen and the full bloom (whatever that meant exactly), and I asked him about it every once in a while. He's pretended not to remember saying that, but Mom gives him the look.

And so last week, early in the morning on September 11, I couldn't wait to get up and see what kind of transformation had taken place.

I took one look in the mirror at my hairline's crown of zits and my bleary eyes and bed hair and elbows (even the best parts of me kinda look like elbows) and knew, if this was the best it was going to get, I was in serious trouble.

So I cornered Dad at breakfast. It was hard to get him to look away from the screen on his phone to talk to me. He didn't want to look at me. Man, I didn't want to look at me.

"Tell me again about the full bloom of beauty, and all that," I said.

"What?" He was screen-eyes, me-nose.

"Maybe it was supposed to be . . . seventeen," he said. "Happy birthday anyway, Addy." He hugged me and kissed me on the top of the head.

I went back into the bathroom. I squinted and the fuzzy me in the mirror looked better. There's my grin—nice white teeth. I have these braids and they're thick as ropes. Maybe there was hope. Maybe I could find a boyfriend too proud to wear glasses. A hot boyfriend, that is. Of course, a hot, spiritual boyfriend. Humble and nearsighted.

Fast forward to now. My phone is buzzing, and nobody is wishing me happy birthday since that was last week.

(Not exactly happy anymore, and not exactly my birthday. F: When my parents adopted me on a Tuesday, nobody could quite remember whether I'd been born the Friday before, or the Saturday. Sometime around September 12 my blonde birth mama and my dark little Mexican Indian dad had stopped in at the adoption agency in Clearwater, Florida, and presented tiny me to the agency, sort of like dropping off a donation at the Goodwill. Then my birth mom stayed just long enough to pick Mom and Dad's pictures out of a photo album, just as you'd scroll through Amazon to find the right color of backpack to order.)

"Hi," I say into the phone. I glance at my Mom as she pushes a warm chocolate chip scone toward me and wonder if she feels like she won any kind of lottery with me. What a shock it must have been to a couple of former hippies to find they couldn't naturally have a baby. So they did the next best thing by recycling somebody else's kid.

"Hi," I say again, then I look at my phone. I feel stupid because the phone didn't ring for a voice call—it's a text message from Lace.

Getme outta here

She's my smart friend. The one with great grammar. This must be bad. I pour myself a glass of milk and lay a banana—the last one—by it.

Need rescue?

Yes—just found out I'm getting kicked out of my bedroom

Out of town company again?

Yes. Can I come hang out?

Come on!

For sure I need to talk to her, or somebody, because I've got something on my mind.

She's the only one of my friends who has her own car, and even with early morning traffic, if she avoids the Plaza area, she'll be here in fifteen minutes. Santa Fe is just not that big a town.

I look across the kitchen table and through the window see the courtyard starting to crank into activity. The cottonwood trees are their own brand of blaring green and gold, and the morning light through the edges of the leaves looks like moldy dust rippling all over the old picnic tables and the fire pit where we hang out sometimes.

Two doors down, the Hernandez kids, all five of them, burst through the bottom portion of a screen door without even opening it. They all have their superhero lunch boxes and are heading toward the bus stop. I kind of imagine their mom is leaning back on the couch, saying "*Ay, Ay, Ay*, somebody will have to fix that screen again."

The rest of the community's kids—the Brown twins, little Elizabeth Pham, and the Baca kids—meander down the sidewalk.

Old Mrs. Grayson is sweeping the sidewalk, not just in front of her door, but everyone's, like she has done every morning since she arrived here at La Paz four years ago. She waves to Mr. Tsosie and tries saying good morning to him in Navajo (she's been practicing), and his eyebrows raise so I figure she's close.

Living in an "intentional community" with an assortment of really different Christian people has its pluses and minuses. On the one hand, we are all together at La Paz for a purpose and we take care of each other. On the other hand, we are all together. *All* the time.

Across the way, Mr. Tsosie is opening the door to

the pottery workshop, where he supervises making the ollas, the clay pots that rich people buy like crazy to help water their patio tomatoes. Past the shop, on the other side of the woodpile for the kiln, I can hear the chickens protesting the fact that nobody has fed them this morning, and I'm pretty sure it might be my turn.

It's Thursday. It is *my* turn. I throw on my clothes and trot over to the place where we keep the animals. The chickens know the sound of the feed being put into the bucket and they start griping. By the time I've filled their water troughs and scattered the feed to some totally ungrateful birds, I see Lace's old Camry pulling into our parking lot.

Don't let her looks fool you. She's all angelic with blonde hair and you could lose your thumbs in her dimples when she smiles, but she doesn't have a great life, and she's definitely not smiling now.

"This time nobody even asked what I wanted," she says.

Chapter Two

"Let's go eat something," I say, and she nods that this is a good idea. But when we get inside my house, a woman is sitting at the table, and she's got a mug of coffee and is eating my banana, and a little kid in her lap is drinking my glass of milk and eating a scone. He has some kind of rash. My mom is talking to her, cooing at the kid—maybe it's a girl?—telling the lady that the clinic won't open for a while, and just make herself comfortable.

"You know them?" Lace whispers.

"No, but I was on a first-name basis with that banana," I whisper back. Lace and I exchange looks that say, "See, there you go." I smile half-heartedly at the guests, get two scones and two bottled waters.

"Stand back," I remind Lace when we get to the

end of the hall. I pull a rope that's hanging from the ceiling and a space above opens up with a ladder that slides down. We climb up the ladder to my secret attic, I call it.

"Sheesh." Lace is looking around my room. "Guess you reached your goal of covering up all the walls." And it's true, the ugly drywall that never looked right even when I painted it is now invisible. Or at least covered up. I've constructed shelves out of scrap lumber and brackets and they are loaded with pottery I've made and books. Since the wall doesn't matter anyhow, I've glued pictures all over it. Some are my own art. I also disassembled several art history books I found at garage sales, and my room is now a gallery of picture-planets all around a sun, and that sun is my favorite, the Mona Lisa. This painting has sent me into an Internet search for everything about her and Leonardo daVinci, the man who painted her.

Lace sidles up to the painting and imitates the smirk or smile or whatever is going on with that lady.

Should I tell Lace now about what happened?

Not yet.

"So who's invaded your room this time?" I ask Lace as she devours her scone.

"An uncle who's Mr. Perfect, but not so perfect that his wife wanted to stay married to him. Divorced him flat after only two years. All my life I've heard about Uncle Steve this and Uncle Steve that, but since he lived in Cincinnati, it wasn't exactly on our way anywhere and he never came here before."

I feel for Lace. At least in my house I'm used to people coming and going, but she lives in a house that's pretty enough to be on Pinterest, and when people from out of town come to visit, her mom goes frantic because they don't have a guest room. She knows the Bible says to be hospitable, but they have a three-bedroom house and Lace's little brother Roo still wets the bed sometimes, so they keep him and his plastic sheets right where they have always been.

"That's what I get for passing potty training," she says wryly. "My room gets rented out."

"Your parents are charging rent?"

"No. Well, at least not that I know of. But he's taken over half my closet, and I'm sleeping in the living room. He doesn't look like he wants to move on anytime soon. Uncle Steve." She says the name like it has too much salt on it.

I have the mental image of her lime-green-and-electric-blue bedroom and her closet of all her sweaters and jeans and school uniforms crammed together next to some guy's suits and gym stuff.

Then I realize that my friendship with Lace is like that closet—I'm the gym clothes next to her fashion-istaism when people look at us. I mean, she's rich and I'm anything but. She's like gorgeous and I . . . well. Braids. Teeth. Everything else is pretty plain.

But honestly, she looks perfectly happy to be lounging in my old camo beanbag chair and licking chocolate chips off her fingers. I just know that it's not the right time to talk to her about what's on my mind.

For the first time, I notice her backpack full of books. She came to stay awhile. I point to my shelf of schoolbooks. She sighs at the signal and pulls out a binder.

Lace attends a classical Christian school where she studies Latin and some ginormous lit book—seriously, it weighs ten pounds—along with the regular stuff like algebra and science. The classes are all day on MWF, so she does homework all day on TTH.

I'm home schooled, and Mom is my teacher. Well, by now, after ten years of it she's more like a supervisor. And where else can you go to school in pajama pants and do all your lessons on a porch swing. And get science credit for going to the doctor and researching the virus you have?

Since I have a whole book to read by tomorrow—on Renaissance art, my choice of course—Lace and I stay sprawled over the beanbag and the bed (except when we go downstairs for a PBJ). Mom comes up to check on us, gives me some feedback on the notes I'm taking, but generally leaves us alone because we're quiet.

We spend until 3:00 studying and keeping an eye on the clock. At that magic hour at which homeschool kids—in waves across the globe—rejoice, Lace shuts the big book with a *whomp*, stuffs in her backpack a report she's outlining about *The Iliad* and how it compares to something else I never heard of, and begins some serious texting. She looks up from her phone as it buzzes with replies.

"I sent a group text to Michaela and ZZ to see if they want to hang out after their soccer practice," she says. The four of us—Lace, Michaela and ZZ and I—met and became friends over a year ago when we all worked together on one of La Paz's community outreach projects.

Michaela and ZZ (short for Zrita Zdunek: In her words, "I'd-like-to-buy-a-vowel-please") kind of got rooked into the project because they were caught texting during a don't-text-while-driving assembly at Santa Fe High and their punishment was community service. Lace came with her parents, and we four girls kind of clumped together that day at our open-air neighborhood health fair, handing out canned food and my Mom's granola bars and coupons for free clinic visits.

At first the other girls were kind of freaked out by the fact that most of the mothers of little kids looked like they were our age, and couldn't speak much English and didn't seem to have any men around. But as the day went on, everyone seemed to figure out what I see every day at La Paz: People are people, even if they're poor or you can't understand a word they're saying. At the fair, everyone was able to understand the word *gratis*—free—for the health care and food.

So Michaela and Lace and ZZ and I all exchanged phone numbers at the end of it. It took a lot of guts for me to invite them to another work day, but I figured I could kind of bribe them, with some of La Paz's famous honey, to work on a flower bed near the beehives; and they came that time, too. Later we all did a Saturday at our food co-op.

From that time on, I knew they'd gotten used to La Paz. They weren't uncomfortable about it at all, even though Michaela's not exactly a church person and ZZ stopped going to catechism and just calls herself a "searcher."

Our friendship kind of welded together when

Lace's parents included us in a rafting trip up in northern New Mexico. There's something about knowing that you could actually die together in the Thunderdome Rapids wearing a Farmer John wetsuit, splash jacket, and helmet. Just imagine Hamlet's dead Ophelia floating in the water wearing this gear, ZZ had said, and we could hardly paddle for laughing.

We just totally like hanging out together, and feeling good about helping other people sometimes, though that's not the point so much these days.

And I have something to tell them that I hope doesn't ruin it all. Today's the first time we're all going to be together since The Very Strange Thing happened, and I need to talk to them about it.

I'm afraid they might think I'm crazy.

Chapter Three

Michaela is trying to fold up what she calls her horse legs (read: long, brown, skinny, and fast) and put them under her so she can sit on one of the old log stumps around the fire pit. She's still wearing her school soccer uniform, and so is ZZ. I'm handing out coat hangers and veggies and wieners and trying to get the wood to stay lit.

"You got any handitizer?" Michaela asks. Nobody wants to take the time to go inside to wash hands. Lace, of course, has plenty.

Michaela looks at the wieners suspiciously.

"These aren't vegan, are they?" She holds a piece up and sniffs it. Ever since I told her Mom and Dad went vegan for three years when they first got married, she tested everything at our house. Never mind that it always tastes good.

"Nope, I bought the pig flesh and nitrates myself," I say.

She relaxes and pops a piece into her mouth. Her eyes close as she chews. Her African-American skin is the color of espresso with two creams and when she closes her eyes and then opens them, you notice how almost scary her green eyes are. But they are laughing at me.

"Nitrates," she says. "Hey, food names can be useful. Here's a randomnicity for you: If you haven't memorized the lyrics for a song in chorus class, if you just sing 'riboflavin, riboflavin, riboflavin,' nobody will notice."

I look at my three friends in the courtyard of La Paz and we're like a little United Nations in the middle of a compound of Other Nations.

There's a cold wind stirring up, and everyone else in the compound was smart enough to go inside for the evening. But this is the only place I'm pretty sure I can talk without being overheard. These are the only people I can trust.

(Love my mom and dad. Great people. Great servants of the Lord.)

(Totally good at least part of the time with me with some of my weirdnesses.)

(Totally would lose it, if I told them. They'd be talking about the collapse of western civilization over this one.)

"So, I wanted to run something past you," I start.

"It's a guy, isn't it! Oh boy!" ZZ is starting to jab

her coat hanger toward me, and I have to jerk to protect my knees.

"No..."

The silence that follows tells me nobody really thought it was a guy anyhow.

"When you grin like that, I'm not sure what you're thinking," Lace says. I concentrate on not smirking.

"I had a kind of an experience a few days ago..." I say.

"And it's not a guy?" ZZ says hopefully. I think she was trying for a messy bun, but her frizzy red-brown hair has escaped and makes a messy halo around her head.

"Not that kind of experience." This isn't going very well.

Lace is frowning at the fire and rotating the coat hanger, but all her food just stays in place, burning on the bottom.

I squirm. "Anybody want more zucchini to put on your wienabob?"

"You're changing the subject," Lace says.

"It's kind of about the Mona Lisa." We had all just come from my room where we'd stashed purses and backpacks, and everyone had seen it.

ZZ jumps up again, crosses her wrists in front of her primly, and does a little mysterious sideways smile.

"You had an *experience* with Mona Lisa," says Michaela slowly, and everyone laughs.

Except me.

"Well, kind of."

If you could slice the silence thin enough, you could fry it for breakfast.

"Oooooookay," Lace says.

"It's really weird," I say, and they can tell by that quiver in my voice that this is something serious, and even ZZ gets still.

"When I started putting all those pictures on my walls," I begin, "I would put some of them up and I'd get this kind of a funny feeling. Like some of them felt warm, and some felt cool, even though they were from the same book."

Still silence.

"And with some of my favorites, when I stood back to look at them, I felt like I could just keep looking all day. Like I was remembering them—not just remembering looking at them, but remembering the people, or the landscapes."

"Déjà vu," Michaela says.

"Well, even more than that. Like some of them were sort of, inviting me. And it wasn't scary at all."

Again the silence.

"And Mona Lisa, that's always been my favorite. When I was looking at other pictures, I'd have the feeling she was trying to catch my eye, like you do when you're trying to say hi to someone in a crowd, but without words, y' know?"

ZZ nods.

"So one day, just after my birthday, I just stood and looked at her. And it was as if there was water all around me, like splashing in my face, but of course there was no water.

"So I walked away and came back. Same thing. Water.

"So I looked a little more at the background of the

painting and there's kind of a river in it, but I didn't feel any wetter looking at that part."

"Keep going, this is cool," Lace says.

"But then the water part starts feeling overwhelming, like turning over on the river raft," I say. "Not drowning, but being carried along like by currents."

"And when you walked away, the feeling went away?" ZZ is the one of us who actually scores in science fair projects. She's already making a mental chart.

"Yes," I say. I take the palm of my hand and hold it in front of my face and slowly turn it back and forth. "So I kind of forget about it for a couple of days and then last week, I'm looking at the picture again and this time, I don't know how to say this, but I'm sure of it, I am with somebody in very old clothes and she is looking at me and it's like she is asking for help. And I feel like I'm losing my balance and dizzy kinda and there's all that water again. I mean, I could feel it, almost feel it, on my skin. And hear it."

"Wow."

"Cool."

"Creepy."

"Oh, no," I say. "It's not scary at all. It's like getting ice cream samples, and you know that even more will be great."

"Let's go up to your room and see if it happens again!" Michaela says.

After dinner we all go up there and I look at the painting and it's like the lady in the painting is looking beyond me or through me or daydreaming or something. And wouldn't you know it, nothing happens. I don't feel even damp.

I shrug.

"Sorry. I got nothin'."

I am more grateful than I've ever been in my life that at that moment no one is making fun of me. Michaela touches several of the pictures and I can tell she's checking if some are warmer than others. Lace steps back with her arms outstretched in front of her and does a slow-spin survey. ZZ looks hopeful anyhow.

But it's after 9, and the girls hug me and I walk them out to the parking lot, and they pile into Lace's car and leave.

I'm back in my bedroom, in my T-shirt and pajama pants, propped up against my pillow. I look at the painting and now the feeling is back. But it is so much stronger than ever before. The painting is pulling me toward it.

I can hear water crashing all around me. I cough because I've just swallowed water, and it's gritty, muddy. I look into the eyes of the woman in the painting and her gaze is steady, trusting.

Everything around it—all my books and the other art—are underwater.

Then my room isn't there at all.

And I can't breathe.

I think I am drowning.

Chapter Four

Whoosh.

I can't tell if that sound is coming from around me, but soon there are more sounds. Water, brown water, is swirling all around me and there's an undertow to it. I try to remember my whitewater rafting training about falling overboard. I think back to some of the rules:

Make sure your life vest is buckled.

I gasp for air, coughing even more, gulp some welcomed air, and try to think. Great, I don't have a life vest, I discover. What I do have is some kind of long slip thing and my legs are in a fight with it. I reach for it and yank it up to my waist.

The water crashes around me. I remember something else from rafting: *Float on your back, toes up, facing downstream.* I flip over onto my back and spit dirty water. I'm freezing.

Ahead I see a widening of the river, but some tree limbs seem to be piled up, blocking the right side. I grab for a leafy branch and to my surprise I can hold onto it, though other limbs poke me. Hand over hand, I make my way toward shore and collapse onto my hands and knees. I've stored up a lot of coughs, the hurling and spewing types, but I can hardly hear myself over the river.

I hear another sound, voices, kind of squealing. I get to my feet, wiping the grit from my eyes, and over the tree parts that have washed ashore I see two women in heavy long dresses. They are holding out tree branches and they are standing right at the edge of the river, trying to fish something out of the water. Each of them has her long skirt held over one arm. I see a what looks like a wet book at their feet and realize it's another book they're trying to snag.

"Don't, Lisa," the smaller one is saying. "It's too slippery!"

The other woman reaches forward with the limb and loses her balance. Though the current is much less in this eddying pool, it must be deep, because once the woman is a few feet away, she begins thrashing and her head goes underwater.

The smaller one is just a girl like me, I see. She begins screaming a Miss Scahlett shriek that helps nobody. I scramble downstream, holding this wet dress thing and high-stepping over the mass of floating tree limbs. I push the frantic girl aside, wade in and once the current starts to take me, I sidestroke against it while kicking and bobbing to find the lady.

I feel a soft brush of skin when my toes find her. I grab some of her clothing and haul her to shore. Once we are there, the lifeless woman becomes incredibly heavy because her dress is soaked, but the girl helps me.

I begin pushing on the woman's chest and after a few seconds she coughs and rolls over. I realize the girl finally stopped screaming in my ear. They both begin wringing out the woman's wet skirt.

"You? You saved my life?" The woman from the river, Lisa, is speaking Italian.

And I understand it.

I nod. It's cool that I understand her, but I'm not sure if the Italian thing will work if I talk.

"My husband will reward you," she says, her teeth beginning to chatter. She points toward a large group of buildings across a field. The three of us make our way through the rows of something planted there, the woman leaning on both the girl and me. At last we go through a heavy door into a room filled with tables, and pots and pans on the walls, and fireplaces. One has meat hanging on a spit. It's a whole pig, with its head and feet and everything. I'm thinking maybe my parents were onto something with that vegan idea after all.

I'm not in Kansas anymore, I think, *and not even in Santa Fe.* But though this had a rough start, I kind of like it. I look around, trying to fill my eyes with everything I can see. Brick walls, fading light from the windows, smoke and cooking smells everywhere.

Somebody calls the girl "Genevra" and two women servants appear, throw their hands in the air and then begin pulling her muddy clothing off. Her chestnut-colored hair hangs in ringlets. Her arms and neck are bruised, and I wonder about that because I don't remember her doing much except scream. She notices me looking and hugs the towels to herself.

Another servant takes the river-soaked clothes off me and Lisa. Mine have blood on them, and I touch my head—it's bleeding where I got a pretty nasty gouge from a tree limb. I look around for men, because once the long white dress thing is off me, I'm pretty much Eve in the garden. No men, whew. The servants bring some steaming water and all three of us are shoved toward a fire and scrubbed and rinsed and dressed.

The underclothes are all silk, but the outer garments are heavy. Nubbly. Linen, I think, like that jacket of my mom's that she never wears because it has to be ironed.

My dress even has pearls embroidered into the front of it. Normally I wouldn't let anyone dress me, but all this lacing and cinching is complicated and it's all in the back. Not a zipper anywhere.

Renaissance, I think. Yep, I know this style of clothing.

"What is your name?" Someone is combing Lisa's long, straight black hair as it dries by the fire and she is looking hard at me. Somebody is trying to comb my hair, too, but my head is bleeding again so I hold a wet cloth to it.

I hesitate. "Addy. Addy Serna."
"So you are Spanish."
Again I hesitate.
"Yes."

To my relief, she nods. I guess I'm speaking Italian. Kind of like the day of Pentecost where everyone heard in his own language, I think to myself. Cool.

"Where do you live?"

I could tell her Santa Fe, but that might lead to some questions I can't answer. So I point to my head and shrug. "I'm not sure." And that's true, because I'm apparently living right now, somewhere, wherever this is. And then somehow I know I'm asleep in my room at La Paz, too. Thinking about this makes my head hurt, and I wince.

"You poor thing. Perhaps you will begin to remember. But we will take care of you, Adi." My name from her mouth sounds exotic. Ahh-dee.

"Have you been in Florence long?" She leans her head back and I see her long eyelashes. Florence, Italy. Well, of course.

"Uh, no. At least I don't think so."

"Then I must tell you about myself, and perhaps it will unlock your memories. I am Lisa Giocondo, and I am the mistress of this house."

I know I am staring. Lisa Giocondo, I had learned in my research, was the name of Mona Lisa. But this woman just kind of resembles the painting in my room. She looks away from my stare and continues to talk.

"My husband, Francesco is . . . as you can probably see from our clothing, he is a silk merchant." She strokes the tiny rolled collar of her chemise. "And this is my sister, Genevra, the book rescuer."

I see that Genevra has put on a filmy black veil that all but obscures her face. As if by explanation, she says, "I am in mourning for my mother-in-law." I look at her in amazement because she looks younger than me, but she's married.

"I'm sorry for your loss," I say absentmindedly, my attention snagged by what's in the corner of the kitchen. Draped like laundry on ropes are the two books, steaming as they dry.

"About the books...."

"You must not be from Florence," Lisa laughs. "Every time the Arno River floods, things float downstream to us. Sometimes people who climb out of it, to the banks, like you did. And things made of wood, which we don't care about. But books..."

Genevra is nodding vigorously. "Books! We love books. I help tutor Lisa's children, Piero and Camilla," she says. "And I love to read, too."

Lisa smiles a big, contented smile. "Imagine being able to live the lives of others, without ever leaving your home," she says. "A book lets you live someone else's life, see things through their eyes, no matter how long ago the author lived."

I wonder if she has any idea of the irony of what she is saying to me. I don't know whose life I'm living, but best I can figure, it's over 500 years ago. And right now, it's really fun.

"You and your husband live here, too, Genevra?"

At my question, she stiffens, just one of those little headjerks that tell you the question didn't set well. Some heat and light seem to drain out of the warm kitchen.

"My husband, Gianni, is employed by Francesco," she replies, and when she says her husband's name it's like she is being forced to peel a lemon with her teeth.

"The family silk business," Lisa says. "Gianni travels much, to Venice, to Cypress, to Lyon, to negotiate for the silk. He's gone now." I see Genevra's shoulders relax.

"Come and see some of our tapestries," Lisa says, and we follow her into a wide hall where bolts of silk fabric and rolls of paper lean in corners. Fantastic tapestries, most the size of my family's kitchen table, hang on the walls. One is bigger than my whole attic bedroom floor. I stare at the brilliant colors—reds and greens and blues that practically shout from the walls. Somehow, I thought everything about Lisa was going to be muddy brown and green.

"You wove these?" I ask.

The two women are silent for a moment, then burst into laughter.

"You're not a weaver, I see," Lisa says. "For those tapestries that are made all of silk, we have teams of weavers—and even the small pieces can take up to eight months." She touches a corner of a weaving with a centaur and lots of soldiers. It is more crowded than ZZ's soccer-team-in-the-minivan selfie.

"A scene from the Trojan War," Lisa says softly.

"Achilles," I say. "The conference at his tent. Getting Hector ready for the faceoff with Menelaus."

She turns and looks at me. I try not to be too smug about a classical education. Well, I just read about that last week.

"Well, then, you'd like these cartoons." She selects an enormous roll of paper from a corner and spreads it onto a table. When she says "cartoon," I'm looking for Spidey or something with big conversation bubbles, but what I see is a meticulously-drawn depiction of the Last Supper, at least as detailed as the battle scene. I realize that cartoon means a drawing on which the tapestry will be based. She waits for me to comment, and I can hardly stop moving from side to side to see the tiny, intricate features.

"This is awesome," I say. "I'm an artist, too, but I've never seen anything like this." She smiles, and I think she wants to tell me she drew this cartoon.

"You are an artist?" she asks. "If you stay with us for a while, would you like to try your hand at a cartoon? Perhaps another scene from the Trojan War? I'm designing a new tapestry and I could use your help."

I can't wait. I start looking around for pencils, ink, my fingers and hands already pantomiming drawing, anything to get going; and she must know what I'm thinking. *Carpe diem!*

"Dinner first, my friend," she says. "And later we will go up and see my Francesco." I hear the tenderness in her voice. By the time we round the corner to the dining room and I see the pig head in the middle on a platter, I've forgotten to ask why her husband isn't at dinner.

After we're seated, I pour a little liquid from my cup onto my napkin and rub my hands. I'm looking for forks and spoons but all I have is a knife. I watch the women and see that if something's solid enough to hold, you do that; and if it's soupy, you use bread to sop it up. Another look in the eyes of the pig, and I'm sticking to the bread and vegetables myself. And I guess this grape juice with a zing is wine.

The other women are delicately licking their fingers as they finish. Lisa produces what looks like a toothpick from a chain around her neck. I ate spinach, too, I think, but don't think I can borrow a toothpick. I see Genevra rubbing her teeth with her napkin and I do the same. I feel like I have food up to my elbow, so I try again, this time under the table, to wipe my hands with the moistened napkin. Great. Now my hands smell like wine too. One of the servants brings me a cup of water. I'm not sure, but she seems to have kind of an attitude.

After dinner, Genevra disappears when we get to the foot of the great stairs. I hear her talking to the servant who brought me the water.

"Maybe she's Jewish," she says. "Wouldn't eat pork, and then all that handwashing."

Lisa and I go up the stairs, and I try to keep upright with all this long skirt swishing around me. She holds one hand to the small of her back and I think that she is more, well, plump than I'd first noticed. The higher we get up the stairs, the more dense the air seems here, more full of smells and humidity. At the top, she pauses and I hear what she hears: two men's voices.

She knocks at a great carved door and we enter. A young man with a beret-like hat is sitting next to an enormous bed with posts nearly to the ceiling and velvet drapes. I think I could be really happy on Saturday mornings if I had a bed like that and could close all those drapes and sleep in. Then I start thinking about how much oxygen you'd need in there and if people ever suffocated and ... when Lisa speaks, I jump.

"This is my husband, Francesco ..." she says softly.

I look at the young man but he's looking into the bed, and I do too. There sitting against the pillows is someone who speaks to me.

"Ah, I finally get to meet this Adi, the extraordinary young woman who saved the life of my dear wife," he says, and I am really confused now. Francesco has gray hair and looks quite vigorous, not sick like I'd expect of someone who was in bed before it even got dark. And he's Lisa's husband? I look from him to the young man and back; and decide that I'll try something like curtseying. I kind of pull it off.

Lisa is leaning over the bed and kisses Francesco on the forehead. Goodness, I think, this man is her husband and he must be twice her age. For the first time, I notice that the bed has notebooks and papers all over the covers, like my dad has on his desk when he's writing a newsletter or paying bills. There's a plate with crumbs and grape skeletons on a bedside table. Nobody here seems the least surprised that the two men are apparently talking business with one of them in bed. I think of how my friends grab a blanket and sit and snack on my sofa when it's cold outside. Maybe that's what friends do here.

"This is my associate Cesco Melzi," Francesco says. The young man rises and bows slightly. I notice that Lisa is backing up, kind of retreating into the shadows of the room. Cesco has dark, curly hair and his eyes are bright, even though they are like black holes and I feel like I am blushing at how directly he is looking at me.

"I hear you are an artist," he says. "And that perhaps during your stay you will help Madam Lisa with a cartoon design?"

I wonder how he knew that, and I say, "Oh, you know, I, um..."

Great. The coolest guy I've ever seen is trying to talk to me and I'm struck stupid. But on the bright side, maybe he's nearsighted. He is smiling a great big smile at me. I curtsey again because I have no idea what else to do.

"Cesco is negotiating on our behalf for a portrait of Lisa," Francesco says. "He knows Leonardo daVinci."

"Have you heard of him?" Cesco asks.

"Well, *yeah*." I bite my lip. "Why, certainly." I put my hands behind my back so I won't curtsey. All the more important because Cesco is walking toward me and puts his hand on my shoulder. I've got on at least three layers of fabric and I can feel the heat of his hand on me. At least, I think I can.

He's close enough that if he is nearsighted, he can back off now before it's too late. But he's not backing away. He is still looking at me. "I am an artist, too. I would love to help you with the cartoon design."

And there's a *whooshing* sound and . . .

Chapter Five

My friends obviously love me, but I'm not getting total credibility when I start telling them about the Even Stranger and Longer Experience.

Well, that's not totally true. Two sorta believe, want to believe; but one is resisting and I can't figure out why.

Lace, ZZ, Michaela and I are sitting in the lobby of a Santa-Fe-cool place called Meow Wolf. People come to New Mexico to have experiences you can't have anywhere else. Like talking to Native American silversmiths selling their bracelets made of turquoise and sugilite and spiny oyster, treasures spread out on blankets on the ground under a porch in the Palace of the Governors. Or going to a Mexican family's quinceañera, the 15th birthday party for their daughter that's more frufru than most people's weddings. I mean, the catered dinners and mariachis and princess gowns and two-foot-high cakes. And of course Santa Fe has Meow Wolf, which is kind of like a psychedelic art gallery slash performance center slash funhouse based on a murder mystery. You want your mind bent, you don't have to time travel back 500 years. Around here, you just go to Meow Wolf.

We are here in the lobby trying to decide if we want to save up for a performance workshop in the spring (that would take some serious money and planning, and I'm thinking college fund is more important) or go for the fourth time to MW's House of Eternal Return where you can seriously freak out in a neon Victorian mansion with secret passageways and scare yourself with the mysteries of time and dimension. Non-linear storytelling, they call it. Boy, would I have something to say about that.

So, I don't think that what happened to me, for reals, is any weirder than the place where we are now sitting.

"It's one thing to watch a movie, or even be in the coolest funhouse ever made," Lace is saying, waving her arm around to the lobby, "but really something else to think that one of your besties has *time traveled*." She lowers her voice to a whisper at this last part.

It's a Saturday, which means Meow Wolf has lines two blocks long to get tickets, and we may not do anything today except talk and stand in line until we get too hungry and decide instead to get Frito pie at the drugstore across the Plaza and look at all the souvenirs.

We wouldn't be the first girls to drown our sorrows in root beer floats and tourist trash.

Lace glances over to where two ladies with gray hair are literally hopping up and down when they get to the front of the MW line, and I think they are going to shove aside some of the little kids.

In the car on the way over, I tried to tell the girls about what happened to me two days ago, beginning with the near-drowning part and ending with the *whoosh* and me finding myself back in my own bed in La Paz. But it was impossible to describe everything—what the house looked like, how the people talked, what they wore, the utter foreignness of it all.

And they have questions. Lots and lots of questions.

"So was the Lisa you met the Mona Lisa in the painting on your wall?'

I've wondered the same thing.

"She does resemble the painting, but not exactly."

"Maybe Leonardo daVinci kind of photoshopped her," ZZ says. When we all stare at her, she explains: "Well, that did happen in history, you know. Henry VIII tried to get a mail-order bride named Anne of Cleves. He had a famous artist do a portrait of her, and proposed long-distance because of the portrait. The wedding was all set up and when Anne arrived, they went through with the wedding even though he told everybody he thought she was pretty ugly IRL."

"Eww," says Michaela.

"And what does 'Mona' mean, anyhow?" ZZ asks.

This one I can answer. "It's short for *ma donna*, which means 'my lady,'" I say proudly.

"Can you speak Italian now?" Lace asks.

I scrunch up my eyes and try to bring back a word or two other than Mona.

"Nope."

Lace has traveled overseas. "There are two things you have to know how to say in the language of any country you go to. The first is, 'Where is the bathroom?' The second is 'no.'" She started saying this with her usual authority, but her voice becomes softer when she gets to the "no."

Some of the girls' questions I can't answer. Like, I know the weather was cool yet there were still leaves on the trees that I had to climb over to get out of the river. But I never saw a calendar on the wall with the date. Four girls with smart phones make short work of that, and we narrow it down to around 1503, which is about the time that daVinci began to paint the famous picture.

"But I didn't meet him, and there was no painting," I protest. "So the most we could say is that it couldn't be later than 1503."

"Whatever," ZZ says. She loves animals, and wasn't a bit pleased when I tell her the only one I saw was on a platter. Or at least part of it was.

"But I didn't eat it!" I tell her. "It was kinda looking at me."

Lace and Michaela bite their knuckles because they don't want ZZ to see them laugh. Her round face is stern. Her hair is escaping again.

Michaela has one focus: the handsome young man Cesco. His deep stare.

"You said he was handsome," she says. "Like dark handsome? Or boyish handsome? Or bodybuilder type?" She is winding one of her long curls around a finger.

"'Help you with your cartoons,'" says ZZ. "Now that's a pickup line. Just how cute was he?"

I shake my head. I don't know how to answer that. All I remember is that his eyes just kept looking into mine.

"Or the dangerous type." Lace's voice is flat.

"What are you saying?" I ask.

"You don't know what he intended," she says, her eyes down at her phone. "You said he came toward you and put his hand on your shoulder..." (here she kind of shivers, and I wonder about that) "...and then you were back in your room. Maybe you were being warned—or protected."

The other girls turn and look at her.

"Didn't see that coming," Michaela says.

"Let's look at the big picture. What do you think really happened?" Lace goes into her analytical mode and I stop thinking about the weird vibes she was giving off before. She's shifted gears: back to her normal looking for answers and solutions.

"You said you knew that you didn't belong there, in that time, in that place," she says, "and didn't you say you knew you were also asleep in your bed?"

Once again, I don't know how to answer. "I can't explain it. It was like being in two places at one time."

"Do you think it was a parallel reality?" ZZ may love horses, but she loves sci-fi just as much. She folds her arms. "The Copenhagen Interpretation of Quantum Mechanics," she says solemnly.

"Say what?" Michaela is rolling her eyes. "Speak

English!"

"Just a theory that something can exist in lots of parallel realities, all at once."

"I'll stick to just two," I answer. "That's confusing enough. But it's like Narnia? Where the kids went from the wardrobe to a winter place with all kinds of fantastic creatures, but didn't really leave England?"

Michaela waves her hands in front of her. "I know you Christian-types really like hobbits and Lord of the Rings stuff, but I just can't get into it. Wizard of Oz, I get that. Alice in Wonderland, that I understand. Both of were about falling asleep or getting hit on the head and dreaming."

"Lucid dreaming!" Lace slaps her thigh. She's the old Lace, on the trail of solving a mystery. "I read about that."

"New research? Sleep studies?" I ask.

"Actually, the idea has been around forever. Aristotle talked about it. He said it is experiencing a dream—while knowing that you're dreaming."

We all think about that for a while. Over to one side of us, a little boy in a neon hat is hanging off a railing by one knee and flapping his arms. He pushes on the reception desk, looking for hidden panels. He must have come here before and is warming up.

"But if it's a dream," Michaela says, "then it all comes out of Addy's imagination, or at least her available, uh, information, right?" I can see she wants to believe that what happened to me was real, but—how real?

"One way to check that," Lace says, and her phone screen lights up from her thumbprint. "You said you'd studied some about Mona Lisa's life, so you would have known if she had kids, for instance."

"Two," I say, thinking back. "A boy and a girl."

"That would be something you already knew. But let's see, what did you *not* research?"

ZZ drums her fingers on the back of her phone. "I know!" she says. "Did you research food they ate at that time? I mean, I know I would have." She pats what she calls her "thunder thighs."

Lace is already googling. "So what kinds of food did you eat?"

"Well, I didn't eat everything—I already told you about the pork. But it looked like some garbanzos, and maybe some kind of cooked spinach, and I remember squash. The bread, of course, kind of tough and grainy." With each thing I mention, Lace stabs the air.

"Check. Check. Squash, check."

"Um, everything smelled of garlic and onions."

"Check. Check."

"Cheese. And fried fish."

"Pizza? Calzones? Lasagna?" Lace asks. "It was Italy."

I shake my head.

"That was a trick question." Lace lays the phone down. "Everything you said, they ate in the 1500s in Italy."

"So it couldn't have just been a dream," Michaela says. "At least, not an ordinary dream. And you know I'm not into the Bible visions stuff. So what's the explanation for how you knew about the foods?"

Lace is still trying to think of another detail we can check. "Trust but verify," she always says.

"Okay, here's the question we all need to know," she says. "Where's the bathroom?"

ZZ stands and points like a tour guide to a nearby hallway before she realizes the question wasn't about here. She giggles and presses her knees together as she sits down.

I had forgotten that part. "Now, that was interesting. It was a little room, like a closet, really, but all it had in it was like a wooden bench. I kept looking around and noticed the top had hinges, and when you opened it, there was a hole—like the outhouses up near Taos, remember?" I say that to Lace. "But under the hole was this big white bowl—no, more like an enormous mug."

"And for the…uh…paper?" ZZ is making rolling motions with her hands.

"Pile of rags," I say.

"Pile of rags?" ZZ repeats.

I nod. "Pile of rags. And nothing flushes."

"A chamber pot," Michaela says.

I imagine any of us who pray are thanking God for toilets right now. I think about the servant who was hovering outside the door and went in after me. I guess to empty the bowl thing. No wonder she had such an attitude, with a job like that.

"So, what happened to you, was it true?" Michaela asks. "I can watch shows about the supernatural, but this is Really. Super. Natural."

I see Lace, the faithful Christian I would expect to jump in here with me to help out, has a look on her face that reminds me of Genevra's veil. I can't read her. What is going on?

I struggle, because I don't understand this supernatural stuff, myself.

"Is it possible for something to be true, but not be what we would call real?"

Both ZZ and Michaela shake their heads vigorously. Nope, nope.

"Well, wait a minute," I say to them. "ZZ, you told me you started loving animals from the time you were little, but it was reading Black Beauty that made you understand horses." She nods, her eyes soft, and I press on.

"But do you believe horses could talk? Or dictate a book?"

"No...."

"But is Black Beauty *true*?"

She thinks about that for a minute. "A book can be true, have truth in it, without being real, I guess," she says after a while. "It can tell a story that has true principles. Even if the events never really happened."

"Like the Bible. It's got true stuff, but it isn't real," Michaela says. "Just old myths, made up way back in history."

Even Lace comes from behind those shields on her eyes when she hears that.

"No, no," I stumble, but I know I have to find a way to say this. "They're true. *And* real. Those people in the Bible really lived. Those things really happened."

I realize that all I have is just my own belief on that. I don't have anything I can tell her that might make her think otherwise.

"There's proof, there is," I say lamely. "I'll get you some information."

Michaela shrugs and tilts her head to the side in a "we'll see" posture. ZZ has just gotten a text, and we lost her attention anyhow.

But there's another elephant in the room of this discussion, and it's not just ZZ's problem with the roasted pig or Michaela's gentle jabbing at me about my faith in the Bible.

And it's not even that Lace doesn't seem to trust what I've been saying about Florence. Something else with Lace.

"Do you think you'll go back?" she asks. "You know, have another VST? You know, Very Strange Thing?" We all laugh at her acronym, but she jumps up and points toward the just-forming line where a new ticket taker has opened a register. She turns to me with her hands on her hips.

"If you can't answer that, let's do The House of Eternal Return," she says, and ZZ and Michaela shove me toward the counter.

"Go back to Florence? I don't know." In the couple of days that have passed since then, I've gone near the portrait a few times and haven't felt the watery feeling again. Not that I think a near-drowning is anything I want to replay. But I don't get any feeling at all.

But as ZZ and Michaela are digging through their backpacks to pay for their tickets, Lace leans in close to me.

"I want you to be careful," Lace says. "You can't be sure if you will go back, but you have to promise me you will protect yourself." Her eyes are hard, and glistening. She grabs my arm. "You have to promise me. Whatever it takes."

I stare at her as she turns toward the ticket counter.

I went through time, and it changed me. Lace stayed here, and she changed too. And I don't know why.

Chapter Six

This latest *whoosh* hasn't put water in my nose, but something else.

One minute I'm staring at the Mona Lisa picture and thinking *what is that smell* and the next I'm riding in a claustrophobically small carriage, bouncing down a narrow street with tall buildings on either side. I think it's early morning. There are people everywhere, and there's the smell. This is worse than any outhouse, worse even than the whiffs you get when going past a stockyard or the Santa Fe sewage treatment plant. Or the boy's locker room at Santa Fe High.

I'm trying not to gag.

I feel a hand on me, gentle. Genevra, the teenager I first met fishing a book out a river, is beside me, and I see we are in a horse-drawn carriage. She puts a square of silk to her nose. To my surprise, there's one in my hand and I sniff it. Potent. The sweet smell on it is nearly as strong as the outside smells. And I think that might not be a bad thing.

On a hunch, I sniff at my armpit, trying to be subtle about it by extending my arm like I'm stretching it. Whew. It's like two stinks are at war there. One is the smoky smell I remember from a five-day backpacking trip to Truchas Peak.

And the other is body odor, the kind that has marinated you for days.

I realize that I smell like the streets outside, smells of humanity and its cooking and heating and byproducts.

I wonder where they empty their chamber pots in a city this congested, and as I look at the mud in the street I think I know.

"You had the same reaction when we came before," Genevra says, and I'm trying to bridge the gap between the *whoosh* that took me back to my home, and this one that brought me back again. "It's always worse when you come to the city," she goes on. "Where we live, there's fresh air. There's not much here. People are squeezed in here."

When she says, "where we live," I wonder: How long have I been here? She's not acting like I just appeared in her life, as I did on the riverbank. Where we live. Like my presence has grown familiar to her. And I've come to the city before.

There is a long space between some buildings and I see what must be a park or a large garden. The leaves there are blaring golden and red. I think about it for a minute and realize that weeks, maybe months have passed since the last Very Strange Thing, when the leaves were green on the trees in the flooded river.

I just hope it's all in the same year, or I'll have a whole lot of catching up to do. And I don't remember anything about the gap. It's like there's a hole in my memory. Or one of my memories.

The horses keep at their plodding on the cobblestones and I'm trying to fill my eyes with everything I see so I can tell the girls when I get back. I see the clothing of people in the streets and it's not the silk and embroidered clothing like Genevra and I are wearing, but something rough that looks like it would scratch. People jostle each other as they carry packs on their backs and poke animals with even bigger packs on them. There are little carts, too. Everyone seems loaded to the max. Everyone is going somewhere. I see what must be a market, with tables of vegetables and eggs, and meat and chickens with flies on them hanging from hooks.

We turn a corner and I strain to look at the horses. ZZ, who says her mutant power is horse whispering, will want to know about them. But they just look like horses to me—not the kind that would rear up with ZZ astride as she throws a rope to snag an escaping calf, but sturdy, dirty animals with blinders and a head-down air of resignation. But as soon as we begin moving away from the market, the crowds start to thin.

We are going out of the city now, and there is more sunlight and less smell. I take the handkerchief from my nose, venture a tiny whiff, and I think I can stand it. I sneak a look at Genevra, and with the sunlight coming through the black veil I can see what looks like a smudge under her eye. We ride along without speaking, both of us looking out our windows, and I wonder if she is just as curious, just as anxious to see the sights of the city as I am. She acts like she doesn't get out much.

The road becomes wider and the horses seem to perk up and walk a little faster, which isn't good news for Genevra and me as the carriage now lurches and shudders when it hits bigger stones in the road. At last we turn onto a dirt road and though it is rutted, it is dry.

Ahead on the curving road is a grouping of houses, large ones like the home of Francesco and Lisa. Another carriage stands outside the front door of one of the houses, and I don't think Genevra realizes what she's doing when she reaches for my arm and holds it tight. It's like she saw Medusa and is turning to stone.

When our eyes become accustomed to the cool dimness inside the house, I try to process the circus of activity that's going on in the entryway. Several men are unpacking musical instruments in one corner and one is trying to tune a big stringed cello looking thing. Two pudgy dogs are roaming in and out of the room, nudging people and sniffing at the musicians' bags and howling at sour tuning notes from the instruments. I try to take a mental picture of them, for ZZ.

At the center of everything is a drop-dead-gorgeous older man with long flowing gray hair. He is wearing all pink and purple; with velvet tights, an embroidered cape thrown dramatically over one shoulder and a jeweled ring in the shape of a bird. I think of how some people dress at Fiesta time in Santa Fe. Or Mardi Gras—I've seen pictures of that. The man is pointing in one direction to the musicians and trying to carry on a conversation with two other men.

Suddenly I can hardly walk. One of the men he's talking to is Cesco. I remember Lace's warning. I realize that Genevra is walking even more slowly than I, and we're holding onto each other like we're headed to prison or something.

Cesco bows to the older man and then comes over to us. His eyes, oh those eyes, look bright, and I think of all the con men and serial killers I've ever read about.

"Ladies, such a pleasure to meet you," he says, bowing. Genevra doesn't respond, and I'm not sure what to do and don't think curtseying is called for right now. Cesco looks at me again. I can't decide whether his eyes are more like laser pointers or black holes.

"Good to see you again, my artist friend," he whispers as he passes. "I had hoped for a second meeting."

I am beyond relieved that, in a past I don't remember, I hadn't yet had the opportunity to completely mess up things with Cesco. After all, there is the possibility that Lace is wrong about him.

"I will introduce you to Leonardo daVinci," Cesco says. And when he presents me as "a fellow artist," DaVinci, who is a whirlwind of activity and words, stops suddenly, and time seems to stand still as he looks at me. His eyes are as golden as a cat's. I'm wondering if he's thinking about the muscles in my face—I've heard he made anatomical drawings of how tendons work. I force a smile onto my face and when it's time to stop, I feel my upper lip stick to one of my front teeth.

As he turns away, I hope his smirk doesn't mean he is laughing at me. But I'm laughing at me—I get to meet one of the greatest people of history, who has a photographic memory, and I've immortalized myself with a snarl.

The parade of people and animals follows daVinci into an enormous room with many beveled windows that look out on the countryside. The light pours through the glass and there are rainbows on the floor. Da Vinci and the musicians must know each other, because with a dramatic flourish of his cape as he removes it, he points to them and they set themselves up in a corner and begin playing music that is strumming and plucking and thrumming on the wood of the instruments. With one word from daVinci, the dogs run to the artist and sit at his feet. His dogs, then. He produces something from a bag and they lie down, chewing and snuffling.

I begin to walk to where an enormous easel is set up with a huge slab of wood on it, and I catch just a glimpse of the front surface, where a cloth covering it had begun to fall off. I feel a hand on my arm. Cesco is trying to smile at me, but he is pulling hard on my arm and talking under his breath.

"He doesn't allow anyone—anyone—to see his paintings," he says. "He says he never finishes anything, he just reaches a point at which he abandons it; and up until that time, nobody can look. Let's just slide over here," his voice was insistent, "before he notices that the cloth came off and he thinks one of us removed it."

"But it was black—all black," I whisper. "He's supposed to be painting a portrait and he starts with everything black? And not on canvas, but wood?"

"Poplar wood," Cesco says. "He is genius. I watch, and I learn whatever I can. He has told me he might hire me to be his assistant next year, and just being around him would be worth the pay." He chuckles. "I want to learn his secrets. But I won't tell him that."

I wonder about the con man idea again.

I turn to look for Genevra. She is standing next to the third man I saw talking to daVinci in the entryway. He has a snarl about him, but I don't think it's from catching his lip on his tooth. It's like his whole body is snarling. His clothing is as fine as daVinci's, but not nearly so colorful. His hair is glistening and lays flat against his head.

He is talking to Genevra, and though I can't see her face, her body is bending away from him like a parenthesis mark. I notice again how slight her build is, how young. I see him grab her arm, hard. I think of how Cesco grabbed mine. A chill comes over me when Genevra and the man both look up and he steers her toward me.

"Ah, my young Adi," he says to me. His words sound slippery, like he has olive oil in his mouth. "No kiss for your friend's husband? Have you forgotten me in the month I have been away? So soon? I made so little an impression on you?" Genevra's head slumps down. I try to think what to say—I have obviously met this man, and I'm pretty sure I didn't like him the first time, either. But I see him squeezing her arm again.

"My dear husband Gianni wants to know about your response to his offer," she says, and her voice is so low I have to lean toward her to hear her. "I mean, it's been months and though my sister Lisa and her husband have enjoyed your visit, he…," she struggles for words, "we, we all want to help you."

I'm pretty sure they are saying I am unclaimed property. What do they do with random teenagers in 1503? Are there auctions, like for a storage building nobody has paid the rent on? I don't think they have artists' retreats, and nobody needs the touch typing skills that dad insisted I learn. And now that I think of it, other than drawing cartoons, I don't have any marketable skills.

I notice that Cesco has come up beside us. "It's either a gentleman or Jesus," he says wryly. I think of the brutal line Hamlet said to Ophelia ("Get thee to a nunnery!") and wonder what it would be like to end up in a convent. I can't even cross myself properly and fumble any rosary that's handed to me. Not an ideal candidate for a nun, even though I do love Jesus.

"Indeed," Gianni says. "And in the absence of your parents, I am offering to negotiate in your stead. I have found a candidate who would like to meet you. A businessman, like me. A man of maturity and experience, who would value your ability to make designs for tapestries." He smooths his hands down the silk jacket he is wearing. I look up into his eyes, and what I see there makes me think about the meat in the market.

With a sickening feeling, I realize they are talking about setting up a marriage for me. Where's a *whoosh* when you need it?

Gianni and Cesco walk away, and I can't hear what they are saying. I turn to Genevra. I can't see her eyes because of the veil. I am filled with pity for her.

But there is no time to talk. Two armchairs are nudged toward one another, facing at angles, and daVinci is leading Genevra and me toward them. He seats me into the right hand one and Genevra into the left. Off to my side is a little table with books on it.

Da Vinci fusses with Genevra's gown and places her hands folded on the arm of the chair. I'm surprised that he doesn't ask her to remove her veil. Then he comes to me and arranges my hands and arms. He puts his head to one side and walks forward and backwards. The music plays on and on.

Gianni drinks several glasses of wine and then disappears. Cesco, though, sits at the side of the room across from the table with the books. When I turn my head to look at him, he pretends that he's not looking at us.

When daVinci goes to the board and begins mixing paints, I notice that he's doing everything with his left hand. But that isn't what's bothering me.

"Genevra," I say, trying to talk without moving. "Why are we sitting here? Why isn't Lisa here?" She turns toward me with obvious surprise and we hear a sputter of protest from behind the board. She turns back to her pose.

"My dear friend, I think your head injury is talking again. Have you forgotten about the baby?"

I think hard and say, "Of course not." (What baby?)

"You have been such a help to Lisa, and she is getting better, but the artist needs to start on the painting. 'Test the light,' he said. We make good stand-ins, don't you think?"

That makes sense, I think. I remember reading that details of the face were often the last thing painted, and even though Genevra looks more like Lisa, being her sister, she's wearing a veil and I'm not. So that's probably why daVinci is having me sit on the right, in Lisa's place, where I'll be looking to the left like the picture on my wall at home. And I'm happy to learn I do have marketable skills here besides drawing and now posing. Babysitting. I think back to Lisa's plump form when we first met. Well, no wonder. She was expecting a baby. No wonder her husband loved me for saving her from the river.

"Your job and Genevra's is to help keep Lisa amused when she's able to sit for the painting, so this is practice," Cesco whispers, and I realize he is listening as well as watching. So my skillset increases: lifeguard, nanny, artist's light meter. And now entertainment. As if he is reading my mind, Cesco hands me a book, and says, "Gianni suggested you read this aloud."

I am delighted when I open the pages—I can read Italian. But I'm not so delighted when I see what the book is: Boccaccio's *Decameron*. I look up and see that Gianni has returned and he is leering at me, wanting to see if I'll read this book which I've heard is way past R-rated. But then Cesco, sensing my discomfort, takes the book from my hand and gives me one of Petrarch's sonnets instead.

I try not to read aloud any of them that are about love, and look up as often as I can at daVinci, who moves back and forth holding a dry paintbrush at arm's length before his eyes as he looks at us and then glares at the board. He's obviously just starting to sketch out the composition of the painting.

"Is he left-handed?" I whisper to Cesco.

"Yes. But more than that, when he writes, he writes backwards, from right to left."

"Why?"

"I've wondered if he doesn't want to smear the ink. But I think it's just because writing the normal way is too easy. When he writes me a note, I have to hold it up to a mirror to read it. Sometimes I think that he thinks in mirror images."

He pats a bag that's hanging from his shoulder. "And that reminds me, I have a letter from him to Francesco." He laughs. "The poor man will have to find his own mirror."

After a while, we all move into a dining room where there are platters piled with cheeses, bread, and fruit. DaVinci sniffs as he fans at a plate of dried fish. I remember reading that he was a vegetarian, and he predicted that the day would come when people would think it was as immoral to eat beef as to murder a person. I want to tell him that he's right, but don't know how to introduce the time traveling thing.

The rest of the day passes quickly. The afternoon light begins to fade, and daVinci seems to tire of his broad strokes and theatrical gestures behind the board. He no longer frowns at Genevra and me when we move, and when the fat dogs jump in our laps, he doesn't seem to notice. After a while, when she and I are laughing at the littlest dog's snores, we look up and both daVinci and Cesco are gone and the painting is shoved up against the wall so that it can't be viewed. The musicians begin to pack up their instruments and

I wonder where all the other men have gone.

"We can't get home before dark, I don't think," Genevra says. "But we should get started."

I try to think of a way to ask about Gianni. "So, your husband will meet us there?"

She shakes her head. "He said he would leave from here for Lyon. He will come back in a fortnight."

I wonder where our cloaks are. Though the sunlight warmed the room, now that it isn't shining in, there is a sting of cold in the air that seems to seep in from the stone walls. I walk across the room and see that there are two doorways and I can't remember which one leads back to the entryway. I listen for the noise of other people and it seems to echo off the walls and floor. I turn into the door on the right and know from the shadows there that I've made a mistake.

A big mistake.

Someone reaches out and grabs me. It's someone strong. He puts his hand over my mouth so I can't scream. I can hear his breath, rough and grunting, in my ear. "Adi."

There is nothing friendly about this. His other hand is around my waist, and it is moving.

I am limp with relief when I hear the *whoosh*. I wonder if I fainted back there, because I find myself lying prone on my bed in my room.

I wonder what happened.

No, I don't want to know.

Chapter Seven

There's nothing like manual labor to take your mind off your troubles.

Old Mr. Tsosie's cat hisses at me as I pull a board from the pile of lumber in the corner of the yard, and I'm so nervous I jump.

This morning I got up and made it a point to not stare at the Mona Lisa on my bedroom wall. In fact, I didn't look at any of the art—just threw around my covers in some semblance of making my bed, grabbed my backpack full of schoolbooks and some clothes, and headed downstairs for breakfast. After my shower, I did my homework outside on the picnic table, and then texted the girls.

Another Stranger Thing. Scary. Will be in the

workshop. Come when you can.

I know everyone is still school right now. I go to find Armando, the Patron of All Things Chicken, a grizzled old man with twisted knuckles and some sort of magic ability with wood and feathered creatures. He's designed a kind of freestanding A-frame coop that can be built out of scrap lumber for a person to raise chickens—and their eggs—in your back yard. It's all about the La Paz philosophy of helping people provide for their families. Armando's eyes light up when I tell him I can help him for an hour or two, and as we work, he tells me of the time when he was a young man that he decided to leave Mexico and set out walking. He had gone twenty miles before someone told him he was walking south, not north. He tells me God was with him, all the way, even when he was going in the wrong direction; that God is always with us when we trust Him.

"He already knows where you'll end up," he says. "Every street address you will ever live at, every telephone number you will ever have."

Armando's words, the sound of the saw rasping through the wood, the vibration of it up my arms, the piney smell of the sawdust—all of this is healing and satisfying to me. And I really want to be here, to be present, in the here and now. I really don't want to be anywhere else. The sound of the La Paz school kids getting off the school bus, the sight of Mrs. Grayson handing them all Jolly Ranchers as they pass by, the coughing of my dad's old van as he tries to get it to start just one more time—this is my life. This is good. This is real.

I put all my energy into nailing chicken wire to the side of a coop, and I leave crescent dents in the wood. I don't hear the girls as they approach and, startled, I drop the hammer.

"Whoa, a weapon," says Michaela. "Maybe I should pick that up." ZZ hands me a consolation prize latte and Lace's brush of her hand across my shoulder tells me I am safe. The light is fading, and it's time to quit working. The girls give a hug to Armando and his smile lights up as they help us put the tools and scrap lumber away.

We sit at the picnic table, sipping on our drinks.

"What happened this time, when I went back, scared me," I tell them, and at the end of my story, they are silent at first. I'm waiting for Lace to say, "I told you so." But she has questions.

"Who was it? Who grabbed you?"

I shake my head. "It was too dark. It could have been Cesco," (Lace nods slightly), "or Gianni, or even daVinci or one of the musicians. There were men everywhere."

"Well, you did come back before anything actually happened," Michaela says.

"I guess God was protecting me," I say. "But here's the thing, though—if I go back, what will I go back to?"

ZZ jumps up and pantomimes karate chops. "Maybe you took him out."

I've thought of that.

"Okay, what if, say, I did? Say I did something awful, like killed him. So am I guilty of taking a human life, because I 'experienced' it?"

"Can't be," Michaela says. "Surely we're not held

accountable for our dreams. Especially something forced on you." At this, I expect Lace to help me out with some Bible wisdom, but she's looking stricken, like somebody slapped her face.

I'm on my own, and something comes to me. "I think you're right," I tell Michaela. "In the Bible, it says that if a woman is attacked, she's not to blame. In fact, it says she should yell her head off about what's happening."

"It really says that?" Michaela says. I open my eyes wide and nod. Score one for impressing my beloved skeptic.

But she's soon ready to change the subject.

"I was thinking about how this is like *A Wrinkle in Time*," she says. "Not just being able to snap between time periods with your, your...," she struggles for the word, "your '*whoosh*.' But it's also light and dark, too—where there is good versus evil. Kind people like Lisa and her family. But there's danger, too."

ZZ nods, then stretches out one finger in the air, making little circles like she does when she's thinking. "Something I don't understand. You enter this, this experience, the VST, by looking at the Mona Lisa painting, right? But this time, when you went back, you didn't see Lisa at all."

We turn and look at her. New thought. Why wasn't Lisa in the Mona Lisa place with me?

I feel like I'm being tested again, like when Lace was googling things about Florence. I have no explanation.

As we talk, I've noticed something about Lace: she's now disengaged from the conversation, even though she offers a quip here and there. It's like she is the one in a different world, and her body is just going through the motions. Michaela sees it too, as Lace only laughs distractedly when Michaela announces with a flourish that if people in Florence call me "Ah-di," then she insists on being addressed as "Ahfrican Ahmerican."

When they drive away, I hear the Hernandez kids squabbling and it's good squabbling—children who tease each other like I do with my friends. I see Mr. Tsosie slowly closing his blinds and I know he was watching after us girls, making sure we're okay. I take my schoolbooks from the picnic table and go back into the warm smells of mom cooking a green chile enchilada casserole for an army and know that our table will be crowded tonight, with people who will have a place to sleep and a full stomach—maybe for the first time in days.

My dad is sitting in the living room with his Bible, finding a little oasis of peace before everyone comes, and it reminds me of Michaela's question a few days ago.

"Dad, I was talking to Michaela and ZZ and Lace the other day about truth," I say. "And we ended up agreeing that good books always have some truth in them—even if there aren't really any hobbits or Narnia."

He looks up and nods.

"But when we said that, Michaela said the Bible was like those books—truth in it, but not 'real.' And I told her that the Bible was both true and real. But when it came time to try to prove it to her, I didn't know what to say. She's all about evidence, proof. I mean, you know I believe that the people who lived in the Bible were real. But—"

His face lights up. "Manuscripts," he says. "It's all about manuscripts." He sits behind his old computer and we begin.

I take notes as fast as I can. This is good stuff. I can't wait to share it with the girls. And I think I just did all the research for a killer paper that'll make my teacher—that is, Mom—really happy. Double bonus.

Mom's already happy, being able to help a sad-looking woman with three little kids at dinner. But after the dishes are done, my mom looks troubled.

"One of those children may have whooping cough," she says. "Dad and I will get the others bedded down at the Hernandez house, but we may need to take the mom and baby to the ER. So don't worry if you wake up in the night and we're not here."

I grab my books and pull myself up the attic ladder, my muscles beginning to talk to me about how hammering and sawing wasn't part of their job description. I shut the attic door behind me so none of the little kids in the house will climb it.

I switch on the light and, without thinking about it, look up at Mona Lisa.

Whoosh.

I'm peering out one of the windows in the studio of the great artist, Leonardo daVinci, and I see that the trees have no leaves on them. The brittle light of a sunny winter day is pouring through the panes, and the fireplace in the room is roaring and crackling. To my left side is Genevra, and her black veil is pulled back so that I can see her in profile. She is giggling. There is a mark on her collarbone, a yellowing bruise. Our chairs are facing Lisa's, and Lisa tilts her head back in suppressed laughter at something Genevra just said about the dogs. At our feet, the two little pets chase their tails until they're dizzy and then stagger toward the fire's warmth.

I look down at my hands folded primly in my lap. I look at Genevra's, and Lisa's—posed in the same position. I look over to my right and see the artist's amber eyes peering intently at us, and then back and forth from the big board where he is painting. There are streaks of paint in his beard. *Maybe he needed three views of hands*, I think.

Lisa, sitting on the right side facing us, doesn't look like I remember her. A rough rash, crimson and flaking, covers the right side of her face. As if she is conscious of my looking at it, she puts her hand up to her face.

"Don't worry," Genevra says. "Remember what dear Adi has been telling you."

I wonder what I've been telling her.

"That the job of the great artist is to capture the essence of the person. He knows what your skin looks like under the rash. He knows it will go away. He would never paint that."

I'm pretty proud that I've been so wise, though I have no memory of it.

"Like God who looks at us through His eyes of love," Genevra says softly to Lisa. "Like your husband looks at you, with love."

I stare at Lisa, and it occurs to me that even

without the rash, she doesn't look very much like the painting on my wall at home.

Lisa's eyes fill with tears. Her voice is low, and I see faint circles of fatigue under her eyes. "I am doing this for my Francesco," she says. "We've come for so many sittings…"

I think about that. How many sittings?

"…and never to see anything, any progress daVinci is making," Lisa continues. "It doesn't seem fair. This isn't a favor this 'great artist' is doing for us. We are paying him."

"Let's keep our minds busy," Genevra says. "Adi, tell me about the latest design you have for a tapestry."

"I'm thinking about a scene from the life of Jesus," I say. "When He picked up children and held them and talked to them…"

I hear footsteps approaching. Then I remember the dark hallway, and being held too tight, almost unable to breathe. Nothing seems very funny to me now, even though it must be months after the last time I remember being in this studio—and yet here I am, safe and sound. When the musicians begin to play from another corner of the room, their music is like a pendulum, slow and rhythmic.

At that moment Cesco comes into the room, and I spasm a bit in my seat. Lisa and Genevra stare at me. The dogs come back, their claws sliding on the tiles, nipping at one another's tails, but there's no laughter anymore, because the women are sensing my panic.

"My dear Adi," Lisa says in a whisper. "You look like you've seen a ghost."

I shake my head, but can't take my eyes off the

handsome young man who bows and takes off his hat, almost like an afterthought. I can see he is trying to catch my eye.

Was he the one in the hall?

Then Cesco walks quickly toward daVinci, a pen and paper in his hand. DaVinci wipes paint from his hands and turns away toward a table where he begins writing.

"I don't care what the great artist says." Lisa's voice is flat, and she arises with one motion and begins to glide over toward the painting. She stands completely still as she looks.

I see the expression on her face. She tilts her head to one side, and then to the other, as if puzzled by what she sees. She shakes her head, slowly, frowning. She looks from the painting to us and back. She begins to smile.

We are signaling her frantically to get away. DaVinci is handing the paper to Cesco, and when he sees Lisa looking at the painting, his voice rises in anger.

"No! Just because you pay for art does not mean you own it!" he shouts. "It is God who sells us everything—but at the price of labor!" He pulls himself up straight. "I paint what I want, what I see, what I like! Don't you know that the painter has the power of the universe in his hands?"

He turns the board toward the wall and pulls it close to it.

"Guard this," he says to one of the musicians. "No one comes near it until it dries. Then I'll take it away." The man puts down something that looks like a viola and walks over. The others keep playing, but in jangling notes as they try to adjust to the loss of one part.

Lisa stands tall and glares at daVinci. He glares back at her.

"I'm done with you," he says. "I am leaving Florence for a while. I have other clients too, you know. I will write your husband another letter later."

He turns to Cesco. "So get me the supplies on that list so we can leave," he says to Cesco, and storms out. "Now!"

Cesco opens the paper and squints at it. He walks to a mirror and holds the letter to it. Satisfied, he turns again to us, and bows. But I see confusion and sadness in his face.

He comes close to me.

"I was out in the hall, and I heard what Genevra said about how God sees us, only through the eyes of love," he says. Then his voice is urgent. "That is how I see you. We have committed our love to the God who alone can protect it. I will come for you."

Then he is gone.

We have committed our love? Whoa.

Then I am thinking about what daVinci said. "So *we* can leave," he said, not "so I can leave." I wonder when I will see Cesco again. I wonder when and how a love between us developed.

As is typical of my life, it seems like I've missed the awesome parts. Maybe it's for the best—I don't even know how to kiss, and I want to try it out with a guy that doesn't require a *whoosh* to be around.

But yet another drama is unfolding.

Genevra has gone pale. She has turned toward the doorway and bustling through it are two men. One of them, I know. Her husband Gianni's presence seems to wither Genevra, and I can see her upper body leaning away from him, a fraction of an inch with each step he takes. But it's me he's looking at.

He walks more slowly as he approaches, like he is afraid of me. He's actually circling, like a cat does before it pounces. His hat is pulled to one side, but I can see that part of his ear is bandaged.

(When ZZ had physical therapy after a soccer injury, the coach kept talking about "muscle memory." And I realize that I have a faint memory of the crunch of cartilage between my teeth.)

I hear his voice, and it is the dark hallway voice of my nightmares, panting a bit as he comes nearer.

"A feisty mare, heh heh, this one," he says. There is no humor in his laugh. He doesn't get too close. "Full of spirit. And her drawings are pure gold."

He is afraid of me, and that's a good thing.

But the man behind him isn't.

If Gianni is oiliness, this man is dryness. He reaches out one hand, and the tendons on it look like pale, purple-spotted jerky. I've gotten used to the smells of people around me, but this one has an edge of sourness that is fighting with some sort of lilac, like flowers rotting outside the chicken coop. It makes me want to sneeze. No, more than sneeze.

He takes off his hat. He is breathing through his mouth. There seems to be more hair coming out of his nose and ears than there is on his head.

Gianni is talking, but his words are bouncing off the walls, like the terrible chords of music.

"And this is the great man, Roberto Tedesco,"

Gianni says. "An artist himself—a master of the art of making money. You are going to be a rich woman and the mother of many rich children." Both the men laugh, and the creaking and cracking of it is like an old car hitting one speed bump after another.

"He has come all the way from Lyon to meet you, and to make your wedding preparations."

Chapter Eight

I never hear the *whoosh* in Florence. Instead, I hear it over and over and over here in my bed, in the middle of the night.

Whoosh whoosh whoosh whoosh. It is insistent.

I realize that it's another kind of sound. It's a cell phone on vibrate. I turn over to look at mine, but its face is dark.

Since it's not my cell phone ringing, I ignore the sound and focus on the other things I've got on my mind. Like how I can get out of marrying Roberto Tedesco's nose hairs. Like how a month or two in Florence could have passed while I fell in love with one guy and got engaged to another guy. A really creepy one. I think back to what Cesco said the first time I met him, about the choices of young Florentine women. "Either a gentleman or Jesus," he said: becoming a nun was the only option for a gentlewoman with no marriage prospects.

I turn over in bed, facing away from the artwork. What time is it, anyway? I grab the phone, push a button, and when the face lights, I see a text from Mom.

Baby was sicker than we thought. Dad and I taking the mom and following the ambulance to the hospital in Albuquerque. Forgot Dad's phone so call mine if you need anything. If you're reading this, it's probably morning and you know what school assignments to work on.

So whoever was calling the buzzing phone downstairs didn't need me. I just want to go back to sleep. I stretch. I doze. I have the house to myself.

Except I don't.

Somebody is walking around downstairs. I can hear floorboards creaking.

Maybe Mrs. Hernandez has come to get a toy or blanket some of the kids forgot. She's got a key. I can go back to sleep.

Except I can't. Because Mrs. Hernandez wouldn't be opening all the drawers in the kitchen. I hear something like a spatula fall to the floor and everything is dead still for a minute. Then the noises resume.

I'll just stay here where nobody knows I am. The first option with an intruder is to hide, my dad always says. They want our stuff, they can have our stuff.

So they can have our InstaPot, I think. But then I realize that if they came in unarmed, they might not be now. Mom's prized chef's knives could fillet a person.

And I don't intend to be the main course. I look over at my phone and know that these old walls would never mask me calling 911. Whoever is downstairs would hear. The police couldn't get here fast enough. Again, I'll just stay put and stay quiet.

But the search downstairs is growing louder as the intruder hurries and becomes more reckless. He or she thinks nobody is home. Probably was them calling the cell phone to make sure first. What are they looking for? We don't even own a TV and my parents' old computer isn't worth stealing. Won't they be surprised to see most of our videos are homeschool subjects. And thank goodness I don't have a laptop yet.

I can hear drawers slide open in my parents' bedroom, some of them crashing to the floor. I hate the thought of anyone looking at my mom's personal things. Can it get worse?

Yes, it can. There are at least two of them, and I hear talking.

Stay put, Addy, I hear my dad's voice in my head.

Can it get worse? Yes, it can. I realize that all my babysitting money from the last year is still in my backpack. I went to the bank and got it out of savings to buy my own laptop a couple of days ago but haven't gotten around to shopping.

And my backpack is downstairs. Maybe they won't see it hanging with the coats on the rack at the end of the hall.

I get mad. I worked hard for that money. I need a laptop. All of what Dad has said about "it's only stuff"—and I'd agreed because I really don't have any stuff—didn't make sense anymore.

I can't stand it. I have to see if they are near the coat rack. There are cracks in the opening of the platform that hides the ladder to downstairs. If I just lean far enough forward I can see the coat rack and…

I'm falling again. Am I falling back into Florence?

I grab for whatever I can, and it feels like my shoulder is coming out of its socket and my wrist twists. I'm hanging in the air.

On my stair ladder. I snag a rung with one foot and turn in just enough time to see somebody in a hoodie take my backpack and bolt out the back door. The nightlight in the hall is faint, but I see another guy and from his position, I think he pulled the rope for the attic ladder. His eyes are wild, bloodshot, crazy. He's skinny as an anorexic.

Drugs, I think. Then I recognize him. Mario Wilson. He and his parents used to live here at La Paz. They'd straightened themselves out, but I heard that Mario had gone the meth route.

"Mario!" I say sternly. "What do you want?"

"Just the keys to the clinic. I'll leave. That's all I want." He does a kind of karate kick and punch that I think is supposed to scare me, but he can't keep his balance and ends up leaning against the wall.

"You blockhead," I say. "There aren't any drugs there, unless you count antibiotic cream and Pepto Bismol and Pedialyte. The doctors don't even leave prescription pads there overnight."

He juts out his chin. He's about to say something when Mrs. Hernandez, with kid #2's baseball bat, comes around the corner. Like most moms, she can move in stealth mode. Behind her are Mr. Tsosie and Mrs. Grayson, not so bold, but backup. They don't have to do anything because I see police lights begin strobing outside and before Mario can make a run for it, some officers have him in cuffs.

Mrs. Hernandez goes back home because she left all the kids in bed except for one groggy 12-year-old she promised a trip to paintball if he'd stay awake for ten minutes and guard the other kids.

"How did you know to come?" I ask Mr. Tsosie and Mrs. Grayson.

Mr. Tsosie points out the front door. "Something woke me up. I think it was the Lord. I looked out the window. Your parents' car was gone, and there were two bicycles propped against the hedge there. I could see somebody moving around in your house with a flashlight. I called Mrs. Hernandez and then 911."

I hug them. I think I'm going to blubber now that all the danger is past. "Thank you so much," I say, reaching around them for a tissue. "God bless you."

"It's what brothers and sisters do for each other," says Mrs. Grayson.

The house is a mess, but I have to answer questions for the officers.

No, I'm all right. My parents don't have any valuables, really, so I doubt anything of theirs was taken. Yep, my backpack had $400 in it. No, I was going to buy a laptop. You see any good computers around here? That's why I need a laptop. Knock yourself out—take all the photos you want. I want my parents to see this mess. Yes, my parents should be back in the morning, at least one of them. Did the intruders hurt me? Nope. I mainly hurt myself. (When I show them how I ended up falling down the stairs I'm pretty sure one of them is snickering.) Can I go back to bed now?

Mrs. Grayson says she'll sleep on the couch till Mom and Dad get back, and I can't talk her out of it.

I text my mom. Not sure how to proceed, I start with the good news.

> I'm fine and the house is fine but kinda messed up but I promise I'll get up and start on it in the morning.
>
> That stupid Mario Wilson and one of his druggie friends broke in the house trying 2 get keys 2 the clinic.
>
> DON'T WORRY I'm not hurt. The police came and all the neighbors too so everyone's on high alert. Some jerk with Mario took my backpack. With my cash for the laptop.

I've barely pressed the send button for the text when Mom calls me. She calms down when she hears my sleepy voice tell her all about it, and that Mrs. Grayson is there. She tells me not to clean up, she wants to go through and see for herself. I climb up the stair ladder, stumble into bed, and fall asleep immediately.

In the morning I hear voices. Mom and Dad are talking to someone. Lace, ZZ and Michaela are murmuring, and from the smells and silverware clanking against dishes, I guess bacon is on the menu. I listen for a minute and when I don't hear any other male voices besides Dad's, I come down the ladder in my pajama pants and T-shirt.

My hero's welcome and hugs from Mom and Dad last about twenty seconds, and I notice Lace fidgeting. For some reason, she doesn't look her usual supercute self today. Actually, she looks kinda scroungy—like me.

"What?" I say to her.

"Did you remember about going to Las Golondrinas today?"

I slap my head. We've only been planning this for weeks. I've never been there and ZZ hasn't either, and Michaela says this old New Mexico ranch experience is really fun. But Lace is the driving force here. She says there's some kind of family reunion going on there and she can't be alone.

I see my mom exchanging glances with my dad over the thought that someone wouldn't want to be alone with their family. I think back to last night, to "brothers and sisters" that are five times my age and treat me so tenderly. I don't ever want to leave them. I want to live at La Paz forever.

I grab some bacon and start to roll it up in a pancake. On impulse, I smear the pancake with guacamole. "Shower and ready in ten," I tell them. And to my mom, "I have a great idea for a persuasive essay: 'Why Santa Fe Needs a Text 911.'" She swats at me and tells me she's packing me a lunch.

On the way to Las Golondrinas, I sit sideways in the front seat and answer everyone's questions about last night, matter-of-fact about everything, including my money being stolen. I am seething about that, though I try not to show it. Maybe the other girls could lose $400 and it not matter much. They're rich, I'm not. But that was a year of my life, and it's gone. And all because we have to take in anyone who needs it. "Could be hosting an angel in disguise," Mom always says. Look how well that's working out for us, Mom.

Something is still going on with Lace. She is driving with arms and neck as stiff as boards. She has sunglasses on and I can't see her eyes.

When she speaks, her voice is flat. "What would you have done if Mario tried to...hurt you?"

"Well, he didn't," I say. "He was too strung out."

"But what if he did?" she insists. "Would you have told your parents about that? I mean, that would have killed them to know something like that."

Michaela breaks the silence that follows.

"Well, it didn't happen, so what's the difference?" Lace's lips grow smaller. She doesn't say anything.

ZZ is giggling in the back seat. "I think it is so totally cool that just a few hours ago you have a drug addict in your house robbing you and today you're talking about it like you're reading a blog article."

"You have to compare it with what else is going on in my life," I say.

Then I tell them about the last *whoosh*, and by the time I get to what Cesco said to me, ZZ is pumping the air and saying, "YES YES YES!"

Then Michaela is pounding the floorboards with her feet when I describe my "fiancé" Roberto and that fat, oily feline Gianni.

"You bit his ear?" Lace is smiling now.

"I'm glad I didn't actually experience that," I say, "I just kinda remember it. Pittooey!"

"Pittooey, pittooey, pittooey!" we all say.

"Now, about experiencing it," Michaela says. "You remember something, but didn't, like, participate in it?"

"Just the feeling of something crunching when I looked at his ear," I say and everyone pittooeys again. "But on the other hand, everyone else seemed to know, but I didn't have a clue, that Cesco and I had been getting serious. Apparently. However you get serious with someone in those days."

ZZ drums on her lips. "So when you looked at him, did you remember, um, any kissing?"

I turn my hands out. "I got nuthin'."

ZZ moans. We ride along in silence for a while. Outside the windows, the pinon trees are squat green spots on the hillsides.

Michaela leans forward. "So, I was mulling over our talk about reality and truth the other day, and how your trip-through-time visions or lucid dreams or whatever they are can be true but not real. And I think that does shed a lot of light on the religion thing—like helps us to understand what's really going on with the Bible. It's a lot like *The Chronicles of Narnia* and *A Wrinkle in Time*…Good stuff. True stuff. But not real—the events didn't actually happen in history."

I know I can't just let that slide by, putting the Bible in the same category as novels.

"My dad and I talked about that the other day," I say, glad for the chance to talk about it again, and trying to remember what I learned from my dad. "I wonder what people would say is necessary to accept something as real."

"Witnesses," says ZZ.

"Well, with the Florence thing, you know I don't have any. And we don't know how real it is, so we wouldn't want to base our whole lives on it."

"Yeah, see," Michaela says, lighting up as if her point has been proven. "That's the way it is with anyone who imagines something and writes it down, like C. S. Lewis" (here my heart leaps!) "or the people who wrote the Bible" (and here my heart crashes).

Oh, how I wish I had all my notes from the other night, when my dad had said the key to understanding this was manuscripts. But I can't just recite information. I believe it, but I have to be ready to give answers for the faith that I have. I have to own it.

I can see that Michaela, for all her blustering, is still willing to listen. She doesn't believe what I believe, but she is willing to listen, and I have to do this right. I send up a prayer. *Lord Jesus, let me do this right.*

I take a deep breath and think about what to say that my beloved friend—and ZZ, who hasn't been to her own Catholic church for years, except for a grandmother's funeral—will understand. Lace just drives.

"Speaking of the Mona Lisa," I say, "let's start with her. Even though everyone knows the painting by that name, there's not a lot of evidence that Lisa is the subject—it could have been someone else. All we have is two written references to him working on a painting of her, and neither are by daVinci himself. And even the Louvre has admitted that they might be referring to another painting he did, so the one there isn't necessarily of Lisa Giocondo."

"Your point?" Michaela says.

"My point is that people accept things as fact with

only a few witnesses, even in fairly recent history. But let's go way back, to the time of the Bible. Let's think about what we know about the ancient world. Like the history of Egypt, or Greece, or Rome. You know, our old favorites Herodotus, Tacitus, Livy." Lace and I know these guys, but Michaela and ZZ have blank looks. In fact, I know Lace knows about the manuscripts for the *Iliad*, but for whatever reason she's not chiming in.

"Okay, how about Julius Caesar?" I say, and now everybody is able to nod. "He wrote a book about one of his military campaigns, the Gallic War, right? And Caesar wrote his book a century or so before Christ, 100 BC. Would we all agree that what he wrote in *The Gallic War* was true—and real?"

Nods.

"So what are the witnesses to that war?"

ZZ scratches her head. "Nobody alive, that's for sure. I guess it would be documents, what Caesar wrote down."

"Right," I say. "Let's google *Gallic War*. Right now. Let's see what documents exist, the manuscripts, of what he wrote down."

Except for Lace, there are busy thumbs in the car.

I'm looking, but not too hard, because my dad and I already did this.

"Hmm," ZZ says. "Looks like there are over 250 ancient manuscripts," she says. "Pretty impressive for old stuff." ZZ shares a site she's looking at.

"But how old is the earliest one?" I ask. "The oldest one?"

She scrolls and scrolls. "Wow. 900 AD. Like a

thousand years after he wrote it."

"But nobody doubts what he said was real, right? Not just 'true?'"

Lotta nodding.

"But I still say it's the same with the Bible," Michaela says. "Nobody has records from that time."

I shake my head. "Check it out."

More thumbs tapping.

"Wow." Even Michaela is impressed. "There are over 6000 manuscripts of the New Testament?"

"Some are just partial manuscripts, but yes, thousands and thousands of them. One fragment my dad told me about, a copy of part of the gospel of John, was made just a few years after John died," I say. "Not hundreds of years. Not a thousand years like Caesar's book."

"John who?" Michaela says.

"John the apostle. Jesus's best friend," I say. She raises her eyebrows. Didn't know he had a BFF, her expression says.

"Okay, so there are old copies of what this John wrote," ZZ says. She tries to soften her tone. "So what's the big deal?"

"It means that if there are documents from around the time of John and the other apostles—the people who actually hung out with Jesus—then people in AD 100 would know who to trust. People were still alive to verify. People who knew John and other witnesses, flesh and blood witnesses. Over 500 people. To say what was real. What really happened."

I know not to go too far with this, so I quit for now. Besides, we're pulling into El Rancho de las Golondrinas. The Ranch of the Swallows.

We're about to step back into the history of New Mexico, and we don't even need a *whoosh* to do it.

Chapter Nine

Once you leave the parking lot of El Rancho de las Golondrinas and get past the visitor's center, you could be in the 1700s. People walk around in old clothes that don't look too different from the street scenes in Florence—all long skirts for the women and men in trousers, leather shoes, baggy shirts and vests. And everywhere you look, somebody is doing something.

In one area, people are carding and spinning wool, and any visitor can try it out. Under another portico somebody is showing you how to make a punched-tin picture frame and someone else is demonstrating how a sorghum mill works.

We stop and each try our hands at making corn-husk dolls. They are really, really ugly.

"You getting low-tech homesickness?" Michaela asks me. She's munching on a piece of bread from a round loaf. Just moments before, a wooden spade pulled it from an adobe oven that's shaped like a giant beehive.

ZZ, the animal lover, giggles. She is all about this place—the burros and goats and sheep especially—until we round the corner and see an animal hide stretched on a frame to be tanned. She folds her arms in protest.

"Where do you think the leather for their shoes comes from?" Lace says impatiently.

Behind Lace's back, ZZ pantomimes slapping her own hand.

It's nearly noon, and we begin walking toward another cluster of buildings. I can hear the sounds of children playing, goofy shrieks and screams, and as we approach a group of picnic tables full of sack lunches, I see two familiar faces—Lace's parents.

Her dad Royce sees us, and Lace practically runs to his arms. ZZ, Michaela and I wave at Royce and Lace's mom Rae. She's laying out biscochitos, tiny anise-flavored cookies, and Lace's brother Roo, who is a mini-me of Lace with his blonde hair and snub nose, is stuffing them in his mouth nearly as fast as they hit the paper plate.

As soon as she's hugged her dad, I see Lace looking here, there, everywhere. Other people—Aunt This and Uncle That—say hi, but Lace is still a searchlight, scanning the horizon. At last she seems to relax a bit and we sit down to eat our lunches.

"I found out something interesting about the Mona Lisa painting," Michaela says in one of her famous randomnicities. "Did you know that Lisa and her husband never did own the painting?"

I pause with my sandwich halfway to my mouth. In all the research I'd done, I'd never thought to find out about that. "Are you sure?"

Michaela chews too much in her mouth but nods enthusiastically. I think back to daVinci storming out of the room, saying he'll send another letter to Lisa's husband Francesco. And Lisa's strange look as she saw the painting for the first time.

And, perhaps, for the last time?

"So did Leonardo daVinci keep it?" ZZ asks. Even Lace is interested in this issue.

Michaela has unfortunately taken another big bite, so we have to wait while she shakes her head and chews.

"You will never believe who ended up with the painting," she says.

But at that moment, she's upstaged by what's going on in the grassy field in front of us.

From behind Lace, I see a tall, handsome blonde man striding forward. He's Adonis. He's Apollo with the sun rising behind him. He's Aeneas dazzling the queen of Carthage. I don't even know him and I know his name must start with an A.

I steal a glance at ZZ and Michaela. They are mesmerized, too. The man is holding little two girls by the hands and walking toward a nearby table.

"I don't know what I would have done without you," a woman with a heavy-looking baby sling across her chest is saying to him. "You are great with kids! Thank you for staying with them until I came back. This one wouldn't wait to eat," she says, pointing to the sling. The two little girls perch on a picnic bench, and the handsome man is showing the mom their purple feet, and the girls are giggling. I remember that over at the Las Golondrinas winery, you can squish the grapes with your bare feet if you want to.

One of the little girls, Mia, begins shifting from one foot to the other uncomfortably. The mom grimaces and says, "Oh no," because she now has both hands full with plates of food.

"Oh, I'd be happy to take her to the bathroom," the handsome man says.

We three at our table are facing Lace, and as soon as she hears that voice, she looks pale. For several moments she seems to be having trouble deciding if she wants to stand or sit.

"Oh, that's my brother Steve," Lace's mom Rae is saying. "Kids just love him."

"I just love those biceps," Michaela grinds the words out under her breath, like she's chewing them.

"That's Uncle Steve?" ZZ asks.

When Lace gets up, she tilts the picnic table, and soft drinks and chip bags go sliding around. By the time we girls have rescued our lunches, Lace is over at the other table.

"NO! Uncle! Steve!" Lace yells, pronouncing each word as slowly as a class roll call. She grabs the little girl's hand. "I will take Mia to the bathroom."

"That's uncalled for," her mother Rae says. "He was just trying to help."

Lace walks past her without looking. She pulls her cornhusk doll from her jacket pocket and shows it to the little girl as they walk.

"Did you make a doll, too? I bet your doll looks better than mine," I hear Lace saying, and into the distance we hear their voices with a back and forth sweetness.

When they return, Uncle Steve is sitting at the table with the other little girl and her mother, and Lace seems reluctant to let Mia go. But at that table there are princess cupcakes, so Lace surrenders her, glaring at Steve.

"Really, Lace, was that necessary?" Lace's mom hisses. "Why are you so rude to him?"

"Really, Mom." Lace looks at her mom with an expression I can't interpret—rebellion? Rage? Despair?

No matter how much we try to get Lace to talk after lunch, she turns the conversation to something else: the old well, the schoolhouse, the chapel, the gift store, and why it's not a good idea to stomp the grapes. She's not looking over her shoulder all the time as she did when we first got here, but seems to be trudging through the tour. It's mid-afternoon when we get back to her car, and everyone falls silent as we return to cell coverage and check our phones.

It's as if that man is in the car with us, the tension is so great.

Finally ZZ says to Lace, "So what has happened with you and Uncle Steve?"

She cries and cries and cries; but not sobbing, rather, what I think are tears of coughing rage and frustration. After a while, she pulls over so that Michaela (the only other one of us with a license) can drive. Only as we drop off ZZ does she say anything.

"I'll text you."

Chapter Ten

When I get home, the house is all straight. Mom and Dad say nothing is missing. Except, of course, my laptop money. They had to fill out police reports and insurance reports all day, so it's no surprise that we have leftovers for dinner. They barely ask any questions about Las Golondrinas, and I'm not sure what I would have told them.

I take the scraps out to the chickens—they like leftovers. Though ZZ and Michaela have texted me with "What was that all about?" a couple of times, my phone hasn't rung or buzzed for a couple of hours. The Hernandez kids and the couple from Vietnam and their little girl Elizabeth, the Pham-fam as we call them, are roasting marshmallows at the firepit. Mom and Dad come out, too. Everyone wants to know about me hearing the noises last night, and falling down through the stair ladder opening, and Mario's karate chops and me calling him a blockhead, and Mrs. Hernandez and the baseball bat, and the police coming; and I act it out in front of them. They all gasp and laugh at the right times and I am filled again with love for these people.

"God protected you," my mother says, and everyone nods. It's what Dad calls "the principle of contravention"—when what could have been bad, *isn't*.

He pulls out his Bible and reads one of his favorite passages, Psalm 124:

>*If the Lord had not been on our side—*
>   *let Israel say—*
> *if the Lord had not been on our side*
>   *when people attacked us, they would have swallowed us alive*
>   *when their anger flared against us;*
>   *the flood would have engulfed us,*
>   *the torrent would have swept over us,*
>   *the raging waters*
>   *would have swept us away.*
>   *Praise be to the Lord,*
>   *who has not let us be torn by their teeth.*
>   *We have escaped like a bird*
>   *from the fowler's snare;*
>   *the snare has been broken,*
>   *and we have escaped.*
>   *Our help is in the name of the Lord,*
>   *the Maker of heaven and earth.*

When he finishes, I think of the flood I was saved from and wonder when would be a good time to tell my parents about Florence. And as we walk back to our house, something is nagging at me, something about Florence, something that was said today. It bothers me that I can't remember it.

And so I'm not a bit surprised that when I just glance at the picture of the Mona Lisa in my bedroom, just long enough to maybe jog my memory, I feel the *whoosh* and I am back.

The dining room of Francesco and Lisa's home is full of shadows. As soon as I see where I am, I sense that it's not just that the candles are burning down, or that the heat of the fireplace is searing our faces, but my back feels like the stone walls are sucking every molecule of heat from that side of my body. I feel like bread in my mom's old toaster—the one that burned everything on one side.

Lisa has her arms around Genevra, who is weeping. Lisa has unlaced her sister's tunic and it falls down from one shoulder. Even in the pale light, I can see bruises and dried blood.

"When Francesco comes back," Lisa says, "I will talk to him. I know he will demand that Gianni stop this."

"He says I provoke him, that he can't help himself," Genevra says, laying her head on Lisa's shoulder. Genevra looks much thinner than the last time I saw her, though it's still winter so it can't have been long. "And he always apologizes."

"He's afraid that if Francesco finds out, he will dismiss him," Lisa says tersely. "I would beat him with a broomstick if I could."

"He couldn't win against the three of us," I say. The women look at me. "We need to stand up for her. To make him stop. Or make him go away."

"And what would we do then?" Lisa asks. "Our parents are dead. Francesco travels. With no man around to protect her, he would go back to the abuse. And if he took her away from here, I could not bear it."

"I'll protect her," I say, and I mean it.

Once again the women look at me. Genevra gives me a smile of such genuine, patient love that I am reminded of La Paz. "And how will you do that, dear Adi, when you're living in Spain?"

My first thought is that I can't speak Spanish, but, then again, I didn't think I could speak Italian. Then it dawns on me: they're talking about when I am married.

I try to think how to ask. "After the wedding, you mean. Let's see, how many days?"

Lisa laughs softly. "Let's see, that would be three days."

This is bad, I think. And I don't know how long I'll be here. I really should *whoosh* right now. I close my eyes and concentrate very, very hard on *whooshing*.

When I open my eyes, the two women are still there, staring at me.

I try to smile brightly.

"We need a plan," I say.

"Let's look at what we can't change," Lisa says, and though she doesn't start with it, I'm pretty sure that in Renaissance Florence, divorce and murder aren't options. "Gianni and Francesco will be back tomorrow, or the next day if the storms don't subside. Nothing we can do about that. They're bringing Roberto Tedesco with them, and they have the marriage contract that Gianni and Roberto signed."

"I signed it too?" I try to ask this casually. Their blank looks tell me I didn't. Probably couldn't. Wouldn't have been consulted even.

This whole thing feels like a snowball rolling hard down a steep mountain, gaining speed and bulk and nose hair as it comes straight toward me.

"And of course Gianni was smart enough to keep you here by taking all your drawings. He knew you'd worked for months on them, so you wouldn't run away and leave them. And you couldn't go anywhere else and sell them."

Months, she said. I feel a great loss. My beloved art.

But actually, now that I think about it, I don't remember any of them anyway.

"And Cesco?" I say, timidly.

Genevra reaches out and touches my hand. "We had such hopes. But no one has heard from daVinci or from Cesco. It could be months, or even years, if he has left Italy."

I want out of this dream. Now.

But nothing happens. A pine knot explodes in the fireplace and sends sparks into the air. Other than that, only silence.

"There was a letter to Francesco," Lisa says. "But it was nonsense. He couldn't read it. I had already told him that daVinci wouldn't finish the painting, and it grieved Francesco so. And then another letter was delivered to the house and when Francesco saw the handwriting, he just tossed it into a box with the other one."

"Did Francesco hold them up to a mirror?" I ask.

The women look at each other. "Why would he do that?"

"Because of the way daVinci wrote. I think he did it just to annoy people. He even did it with notes to Cesco."

"I'll go get the letters," Lisa said, and in a few moments she returns.

"Maybe when Francesco comes back, he will have cooled down and want to know what's in the letters," she says. "This is the first one."

With a candle in one hand and the letter in another, I face a mirror. It is addressed to Francesco, and says things like art is the queen of all sciences and wisdom is the daughter of experience and a man should not paint to the standards of others. In other words, "Fuggettabout your painting!"

"I had concluded as much," Lisa says. "So why did he write the second letter?" She hands it to me.

I can't read it without the mirror. I guess daVinci thought they'd know to use one after deciphering the first letter.

But when I hold it up, I can't believe my eyes. It's to Francesco, but in very small writing, there is another name as recipient.

My hands are trembling.

But at that moment a terrible racket of knocking starts at the front door. Servants are running from side halls. Once inside, two wide-eyed men are shaking rain from their coats and bowing over and over.

"We have terrible news," they say. "Terrible news. We bring our deepest sympathy."

I really want to know what's in the letter.
I even want to hear the terrible news.
Whoosh.

Chapter Eleven

M: Here's ur randomnicity 4 the day. A Turkish proverb. No matter how far u have gone down the wrong road, turn around

Z: U need that, after we saw how u drive. IMHO

M: Watch it

M: Lace, Addy, u guys up?

Z: Crickets

Z: Ur not the only 1 w randomnicities. Here's mine 4 the day from Golda Meir

M: Who?

Z: Prime minister of Israel or something

Z: Don't be humble…you're not that great

M: Say what?

Z: It's the quote from Meir

M: Whew. Thought I was going 2 have 2 come over and spank 1 of your horses

Z: Hahahahah

M: Poor u. Having 2 laugh w letters, since we banned u from using emoticons n r group texts

Z: Just bc I used 50 that 1 time

A: Hi!

A: Been busy. Roosters and reports

M: ???

A: More police reports. And chicken issues

Z: U r the only person I know w chicken issues

A: So my question of the day. If I get married in Florence, am I still a virgin?

Z: Whoa

M: Double whoa

M: Another whoosh? What happened?

A: Nothing yet. Wedding in 3 days

Z: Not Cesco?

A: Not Cesco

M: Arggggggggggh

L: Come now right now

L: Called 911

L: Need you

Chapter Twelve

My dad drives as fast as Santa Fe's narrow streets will allow, and by the time we get to Lace's house out near the Opera, there are two police cars in front of her flat-roofed adobe duplex. And a lot of people in the small front yard. People from next door are barbecuing on a grill, but they're watching too.

ZZ and Michaela are hugging Lace. She is sobbing and has Roo in her arms.

To my surprise, two policemen are restraining her dad Royce, and he's trying to get free. They are just holding onto his arms. No handcuffs, no stun guns.

Lace and Roo reach for their dad.

Another officer is talking to Uncle Steve, who is leaning up against the garage door, his arms folded. I think he's trying to look GQ, but that's not working for him anymore.

"She's hysterical," Uncle Steve says, waving his arm toward Lace. "Kids make up stories. Everyone knows that."

Another car screeches around the corner, and Rae, Lace's mom, jumps out of it. She looks from person to person, not sure what to do. My dad goes and stands by Royce, and I run to Lace and the girls.

Lace wipes her eyes.

"I reported Steve."

He hears this, and points to me.

"Like this kid, this Addy. She thinks she travels through time. Kids and their stories."

"I thought I could trust him," Lace whispers to me. "At first. I told him things."

I shrug. "That doesn't matter at all," I say, and she tells me thank you with her eyes.

A lady is standing near us, and she starts walking toward Rae. She takes Rae by the arm, gently, and faces her away from the garage door.

"Tell them, sis," Steve is yelling at Rae. "Tell them I didn't do anything."

The lady is showing Rae a badge. As she talks, Rae twists around and looks back and forth from Lace to Steve.

Lace is sobbing again. "He. . .he said you would never believe me. He said he would. . . kill dad and Roo if I told you what he did to me." Lace and Rae hold each other for a long time, then Rae steps back and puts one hand on each of Lace's shoulders. She leans down. They are eye to eye.

"I may have been blind and stupid," Rae says, "but know this: I will *always* believe you."

Rae stands up straight, and as the woman officer begins talking to Lace, she turns slowly. She and Royce lock eyes.

Here's another mom who knows how to move in stealth mode: she almost makes it to Steve before the lady officer grabs her and pulls her back.

After Rae allows the officer to escort her back to her husband and agrees to restrain herself, the officer goes over and talks to Steve for a minute. She writes some things down, then he walks to his car and drives off.

I look at ZZ and Michaela, and tilt my head to the inside of the house. We know just what to do. It doesn't take us two minutes to haul all Steve's clothes out of Lace's closet and onto a pile in the front yard.

For the first time in a long time, I see the old Lace smiling.

She smiles even more when the neighbor who was barbecuing offers lighter fluid and a match to Royce. He squirts it all over the pile of clothes and sets it on fire.

Chapter Thirteen

Whoosh.

Now, I'm confused.

It's been days since Steve was finally arrested, and I've finally worked up the courage to look at the picture on the wall of my bedroom.

The *whoosh* happens, but after it I'm still looking at the painting.

But not the painting on my wall. I squint. Almost, but not.

Suddenly many things become very clear in the sun-drenched room where I now sit.

The mountains in the background of this painting are not the drab browns and olives, but snow-capped, gleaming in the sun. The sky is a brilliant blue. The lake is a profound and multi-layered azure like the Blue Hole of Santa Rosa.

The young woman's hair is chestnut, fine and wavy. I know that hair. Not Lisa's straight black hair.

And I know that face, with the gaze that is both shy and direct, challenging and trusting. Her cheeks are pink as if she has been laughing, and just the memory of a wriggling puppy or a gentle joke still lingers there.

Her neck and shoulders have no bruises, no scars.

She's wearing the same black mourning veil, but it's pushed back on her hair, framing her face, and the sleeves of her blouse are a joyous red.

It's the best version, the happiest memory. I think back to what she said: "Like God who looks at us through His eyes of love."

I look at her hands, folded in front of her like when we posed, keeping her sister company while we thought Lisa was being painted by daVinci.

I look down at my own hands, and I can see the veins on the back of them, and brown spots. I stretch them open and see that the knuckles don't look right, kind of torqued. They don't look young.

Someone is standing behind me. I feel his hands on my shoulders, and recognize the familiar, welcome heat, that solidity and strength.

Cesco steps around my chair and sits down across from me. It is the same Cesco I met as a young girl, but his hair is now white. His eyes, though, are still dark as onyx.

"You look as though you've never seen me before, my love," he says gently.

I don't know what to say, so I look back at the

painting.

"DaVinci had his faults," Cesco says, "but so much for which we loved him, so much genius that we forgave him. He saw the tenderness, the beauty in Genevra that Gianni never did. He immortalized it. And then he knew he couldn't give the painting to Lisa and her husband."

I know—though I don't know how—that this is the last time I will be here in Florence. And there will be too many questions unanswered.

So I lean across to Cesco and take his hands. His hands are old, too, and I see paint under his fingernails and on his cuticles. I look back into those eyes.

"Let's go back and remember those days," I say. "Pretend I don't remember. Tell me about how you came to get me."

He smiles and his eyes look far away, to the past.

"The worst days of my life, God turned to the best. When I did not hear from you after I sent the letter to Francesco's house, I felt such deep despair. Everything started happening so quickly, and Leonardo heard news that you were going ahead with the wedding to Roberto Tedesco. I couldn't understand why you wouldn't wait for me to return.

"And then God, the great God of the universe, took charge. As soon as I heard that the ships carrying Gianni and Roberto were lost in the storm, I felt hope again. Of course there was thought of a rescue, but it was days before we knew their fate."

"Poor Genevra," I said. "Waiting and wondering."

"But you found my letter inside the one Leonardo wrote to Francesco. You wrote to me and my heart soared. I rode as fast as I could back to Florence, and the wedding preparations that were already done—well, we tried not to find too much humor in the fact that Roberto paid for our wedding."

Our wedding. I close my eyes so that he won't suspect all the emotions that are going on inside my head. He leans back in the chair, still reminiscing.

"Bless Lisa and Francesco for their offer to keep Genevra with them since she was now widowed, but of course none of us could know she wouldn't live through the next winter."

We look again at the painting.

"But see! We have this to remember her, and this picture of our lives."

He points to another wall. A tapestry hangs there, and it's the design I wanted to draw of Jesus surrounded by at least a dozen children. Cesco is pointing, his finger caressing the face of a boy.

"Our son Orazio," he says, "just how he looked when he was a little boy."

I stare at the face of a boy that looks very much like Cesco.

"And his wife. And all these," Cesco sweeps the tapestry with his finger, "all those ten grandchildren, each a gift from God."

I remember something I've heard my dad say, about the satisfaction of a life well-lived.

Cesco is pointing to each child's face. I don't remember any of their names. This is a lot to take in.

But then I know I don't have to, because I know that sound, and I know what it means; though this last time I wanted to stay just a moment more.

Chapter Fourteen

Lace, Michaela, ZZ and I are sitting in the dining room of the La Fonda Hotel, downtown, pretending we're rich tourists who aren't all that hungry. We could each afford to buy a soda and share an appetizer plate of pork carnitas with jalapeno salsa and orange-achiote syrup. I keep expecting ZZ to go rogue vegan on me at some point, but food like this gets in the way of her principles. Kinda like mom's fudge does to my diets.

We're talking about my last trip to Florence.

"So why does this feel like a funeral?" Michaela asks.

"Maybe because everyone there is dead," ZZ says.

Hadn't thought of that. But if it all really happened, then somewhere in the past, Adi, the wife of

Cesco, must have passed away...

I wonder to myself—what advice would she have for me? What would she tell me was really important in life? I think about something I read in the book of Proverbs, about a woman who is clothed in strength and dignity, who can laugh at the future.

"Score another one for Addy, though," Michaela says, interrupting my thoughts. "I never did get to tell you that I looked it up and found out that Cesco Melzi went to work for Leonardo daVinci, and actually ended up with the Mona Lisa painting."

"Except it wasn't of Lisa," I say. "They were sisters, that's true, and they did resemble each other. That tricky daVinci loved to do things in mirror images. All the time that Genevra and I were sitting across from Lisa, thinking we were keeping her entertained, daVinci was painting Genevra. In a mirror image, of course."

Michaela points to her phone. "And in France and Italy, people don't call the painting 'Mona Lisa,' like we do. They call it some version of her last name which also means 'the merry woman.' Kind of a play on words."

"But what about Genevra's veil, and those bruises?" ZZ says.

"I remember her pushing the veil away from her face—for some reason, she wasn't afraid of him seeing the bruises," I say, thinking back. "I wonder if daVinci could see the pain she had, and he made a decision that she was the woman he wanted to paint, to have her remembered with that smile of contentment on her face, being with people she loved and who loved her."

"I can understand that," Lace says, and looks at each of us. She's been in counseling for a couple of weeks now, and we try not to ask too many questions, but let her bring it up. She's already told us that her counselor says most predators aren't the stranger-in-the-hoodie, they're somebody you already know, the relative or coach or other adult that you and your parents trust. In fact, that trust lets them get away with a lot.

"You guys are helping me so much," she says. "And my parents. We are all dealing now with a sense of betrayal. Like being sold out by someone who's supposed to care about you."

"How do you ever get over that?" Michaela asks.

"Actually, something my dad brought up," Lace says. "There's a story in the Bible about a guy about our age, named Joseph, whose brothers actually kidnapped him and sold him."

"No way," ZZ says.

"Why?" Michaela asks.

"Because he had these dreams that he was someday going to rule over them."

"Aha! Dreams!" Michaela says.

"And then years later, when they all meet up again, the brothers are really sorry—especially since Joseph became really powerful, almost like a king. Naturally, they're afraid Joseph is going to find a way to get even. But Joseph tells them that what they meant for evil, God meant for good. God would bring something good out of the situation."

"You think Steve is going to say he's sorry?" I ask.

Lace shrugs. "My counselor tells me not to expect that. But what you said about Genevra, that means so much to me," she says. "God cares about what happened to me, He knows the bruises on my heart are there, but he doesn't want me to be remembered that way. I don't want you guys to think of me as 'what Steve did.'" She makes quotation marks in the air. "It may take a while, but I really want to see what good God can bring out of that situation."

ZZ looks very serious. She waves her arm dramatically and pulls her legs up until she is cross legged in her chair. She steeples her hands.

"Scarab beetles are born out of camel dung," she says, rocking back and forth, and Lace punches her in the shoulder. Then I punch her too.

"We have to go on, making our own new memories," Michaela says. "People make artwork out of things other people just toss aside, and it's beautiful. At La Paz, you make chicken coops out of old lumber and people are able to feed their families. I mean, here we are, living in a whole city that's mainly built out of adobe mud!"

"Good point, Michaela," I say, impressed and encouraged that my skeptical friend is starting to grasp the concept of God's providence. And then something else occurs to me: "Come to think of it, even the Mona Lisa itself is an illustration of good coming out of bad. I remember reading that before the early 1900s it wasn't that famous at all—it was just hanging in the middle of a bunch of other paintings in the Louvre. Then a museum worker stole it and kept it in a closet for two years—really interesting story—and after that it became the most famous painting in the world. Which never would have happened if it hadn't been stolen."

"Do you think you'll have any more VSTs with artwork?" Lace asks. "You said you got a strange feeling from some of the other paintings."

I don't tell them, but lately another of my paintings is trying to get my attention.

"I've thought about that myself," I say. "Don't know. But yesterday I read a killer quote from Leonardo daVinci."

Everyone leans forward.

"'Once you have tasted the taste of sky,'" I tell them, "'you will forever look up.'"

Stay tuned for more *Into the Art* books from Latayne C. Scott!

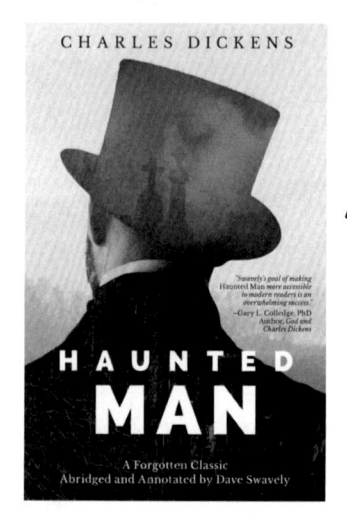

HAUNTED MAN

by Charles Dickens | 140 pages

A Forgotten Classic

*Abridged and Annotated by
Dave Swavely*

A college professor named Redlaw is a good man plagued by bad memories of a traumatic childhood, compounded by a terrible betrayal and loss during his young adulthood. When an ethereal demonic doppelganger of himself appears and offers to wipe away those memories, Redlaw eagerly accepts, and also receives the ability to spread this "gift" to others.

Featuring the breathless suspense, colorful characters, and witty humor that has made Dickens such a beloved author, the story also tackles some of the deepest philosophical and theological questions ever raised in his writings. His answer to "the problem of evil" is of both literary and religious interest.

"Swavely's goal of making Haunted Man more accessible to modern readers is an overwhelming success."
     –Dr. Gary L. Colledge (PhD, University of St. Andrews, author of God and Charles Dickens

NEXT LIFE: A Novel

by Dave Swavely | 125 pages

One Christian's adventure of a lifetime
...in the NEXT LIFE!

What happened to Tim Carler is so hard to believe that he had to call his story a novel to keep from being mercilessly mocked (or locked up for his own safety). But ironically, his account rings true in a way that other "heaven tourism" books do not. Unlike those supposedly non-fiction titles, there's nothing in this one that contradicts Scripture.

After the shock of finding his soul in the Intermediate State, the surprises multiply as Tim finds out who's there, who's not, and how different heaven is from our common conceptions. In a dimension not bound by time, he is sent on missions into the past where he meets some extraordinary everyday people, as well as famous ones like the Jewish Patriarchs, Adolf Hitler, and two Victorian Charleses—Spurgeon and Dickens.

Reminiscent of *A Christmas Carol*, but with more gospel content. It's a *Pilgrim's Progress* where the journey takes place in the life to come rather than in this one.

Visit

CruciformPress.com

for more Cruciform Fiction books as well as

*Bible Studies for Women
by Keri Folmar*

and more than sixty Christian titles from top authors such as

**John Piper
Tim Challies
Jerry Bridges**

and many more